LOST:

The Time Travel Romance
That Started It All

By

USA Today Bestselling Author

Dani Haviland

LOST: the epic time travel romance and how it changed lives in the 21st century.

Chill Out!
Books

Copyright © 2021

Dani Haviland and Chill Out! Books

Book description

LOST: the time travel romance that fascinated the world.

Millions were Obsessed - Inspired - and Consumed with the loves, lives, and even languages spoken in LOST.

Enjoy snippets from the epic tale and how the story forever changed the lives of men and women from Alaska to the UK.

The prequel to The Fairies Saga and Arlie Undercover also introduces characters from That Twin Thing and Triplets: Three Aren't One, four worlds where heroes and villains from the Catenated Universe match wits and fall in and out of love.

Dedication

This book is dedicated to all the passionate friends of fiction throughout the world. What a boring place we'd have without Disneyland, Comic Con, and all those Outlander Obsessed fanatics!

Praise and Awards

USA Today Bestselling Author

Kindle Top 10 Bestselling Author

Amazon Top 10 Historical fiction Author

Amazon Top 10 Biographies and Memoirs Author

Amazon Top 10 Short Story Anthologies and Collections Author

Amazon Top 10 History of Women in the American Civil War Author

Amazon Number One in Black and African American Science Fiction
Author

Amazon Top 10 United States Drama and Plays Author

Amazon Top 10 Organized Crime Thrillers

Amazon Top 10 Two-hour Romance Reads

Amazon Top 10 LGBT Mysteries Author

Amazon Top 10 Holiday Romance

Amazon Number One Weddings Author

Amazon Top 10 Satire Author

Amazon Top 10 Romance Anthologies

"Touches of humor…lively romance…intricate plot…and lots of action." **Judge, Writer's Digest Self-Published e-Book Awards**

Great descriptions, interesting heroine who is capable of surviving in (let us say) a challenging set of elements, and a fun twist when (SPOILER) she meets some very familiar literary friends. You never know what's coming around the next corner in this book! I also really liked the historical element. **BooksAreLife**

Chapter 1: Greed and Deception

August 2011
London, England

Clotilde demurely excused herself from the table then strode into the restroom of London's finest eatery and locked the door. She withdrew the hidden bundle of keys she'd purloined from her clueless boyfriend, grinning with pride at her deception. James Melbourne was good-looking, soon to be a member of the House of Lords, and best of all, rich. Too bad she didn't care for him. Randy was her *real* boyfriend, and she didn't need the hassle of two men.

She held the keyring in the air, inspecting the top of each key for the right shape. Her brother assured her this would work. She fumbled through her purse for the half dozen small tins he'd given her and laid them out on the lavatory counter. Out of curiosity, she slid the top off one and sniffed it. It smelled like glue but looked like a great glob of pre-chewed gum. She selected the two keys on the ring that looked like they'd fit a door.

Ooh. A padlock key. I'll take an impression of that one, too. Who knows? Maybe there's a treasure chest around somewhere.

A quick push of one flat side of the key into a container, then the reverse side into a separate tin and one key was copied. By the time she got to the last impression, she felt like a pro. Big brother JB would create plaster molds from the goop, then finish the project by pouring hot metal into them, handing her the finished products in two days.

Once she had the keys to the Melbourne Mansion and awestruck James Melbourne's heart, she would be on the fast track to riches. A rushed engagement and elopement – followed by accusations of physical abuse or whatever she thought would work – and she'd file for divorce. Once she got her humongous settlement, she would be set for life. Maybe she'd be gracious and chuck a few quid big brother's way, but this was her plan, not JB's. Daddy would be so proud of her.

***

Three days later

It was official. She had the ring and got him to say the words. Now her fiancé was gone – Thank God – sent on a business trip to America by his eccentric grandfather. Silver-haired Lord Martin Melbourne wasn't dim enough for others to dismiss entirely – hard to do since he was a member of the House of Lords and automatically deserved respect – but he was undeniably living in his own private world, operating on a different frequency.

It seemed like years ago, but it was only two weeks earlier that Clotilde had happened upon James and learned of the Melbourne fortune. With three generations of men in the family, surely one would be an easy target. The senior in the family was Lord Martin Melbourne. Rumor was he wasn't subject to the wiles of either clever or gorgeous persons of the fairer sex. She'd have to drop to the next generation and hope to get the money from his progeny via divorce rather than becoming a widow.

Lord Martin did have a son and a swayable one at that: Bruce. Conveniently for her, they had a mutual friend, one she could easily compel with either a threat or a promise. A few choice words regarding his gambling debts and the man quickly promoted her as a near saint to Bruce and his inner circle.

Unfortunately, Clotilde didn't know– but everyone else did – that the heir to the family title was homosexual and didn't care for or about women. He also didn't want to take on the inherited responsibility of a seat in the House of Lords. A world-famous mountain climber, he was only out to please himself...and maybe a boyfriend or two. Another lost opportunity.

That left only one person for Clotilde to latch onto: the youngest generation, Bruce's only son, James.

Youthful and good looking, James was naive in the ways of the world. Extremely bright, he had attended university at an early age and missed out on the social life needed to attain full maturation. This was ideal for Clotilde. She 'bumped into him' at a restaurant and started a casual rapport. Piece of cake. She was in and had his interest. A few provocative encounters, working him into a frenzy before leaving him wanting, ensured he'd be back. Teasing was her specialty. Make men hungry but don't give them what they want. She was the only one in her world she was going to please.

Now, Bruce was missing. She had no part in his disappearance, but it was a fortunate occurrence for her. Apparently, he'd fallen off some mountain peak – or maybe it was down an icy crevasse – on the other side of the world. It didn't matter which. He was out of the picture and she was engaged to his son. Once Bruce was legally declared dead, James would be bumped up to next in line to the Melbourne fortune.

Lord Martin was still alive as far as anyone knew, but if he didn't make an appearance soon, James would have the title and sole access to the millions. The man-child was her portal to the family fortune. Investing her wiles in him was truly a stroke of genius, even if it did make her real boyfriend jealous. Randy would get used to it. It wasn't as if she was ever going to sleep with James, even after they were married. She had dozens of excuses, at least enough to use until it was time to sue for divorce.

Ah, only a short time and she would *truly* be Lady Clotilde. She wouldn't be lying when she introduced herself as such to valets, vendors, or anyone else who didn't know the Melbourne name. Soon, she would be somebody!

The house was empty now, the staff sent on a generous holiday by the missing master of the house via a fabricated phone call to her. She had the stately, echoing halls all to herself. First stop, James's office. She verified it was his by the picture he had mentioned more than once. The focal point of the room was a massive portrait of an ancestor, part of his fascination with the past.

Clotilde pushed the stool closer to the picture of an eighteenth-century Melbourne. Or was that seventeenth or nineteenth? It didn't make a difference. The man was dead. Looked like a queer with his dark curly ponytail resting on his shoulder and those full rosy lips. Not that it made a difference. He wasn't the one she needed to seduce to get access to the family fortune. She already had the target and was locked on, her prey helpless and hers to use.

She tried lifting the corner of the portrait to see if the safe was behind it, but it was too heavy. Instead, she stuffed her cell phone in the narrow opening between it and the wall, then snapped a shot. She brought the phone back out, grunting at the inconvenience, and pinched the screen, enlarging the flash-lit image. "Ah, there it is."

Determined to get it down by herself, she lost her balance and almost fell trying to heft the heavy-framed portrait. She tried again before realizing it was mounted on hinges. Grasping it by the right edge, she swung it open like a big book.

"Now, that was clever. It's a good thing no one knows I have a key to the place. Those dolts were all too eager to believe my story of how the old coot had given them two days off with pay to mourn Bruce. Not a bad plan, eh?" She grinned in satisfaction. "Who said I was the dumb sibling? Oh, yeah. It was you, wasn't it, JB?"

Big brother James Bradford was a gentlemen's gentleman at White's House of Chocolates, an exclusive club for the old monied men of England. He was privy to many overheard conversations –

4

secrets, stock tips, and rumors – but was too slow to know what to do with the information. "Or maybe just too ignorant. You're a dull tool, but sometimes a cricket bat is needed, not a razor."

Using the hint Randy had given her, Clotilde pulled down on the safe's handle first. Messing with the combination might lock it if it was already open.

Click

"Eureka!" Clotilde shrieked, then cowered. No one was supposed to be here, but some servants lived on the grounds. She didn't want to let anyone know she was here. Or that she had copied the keys on James's keyring.

Tiptoeing on the stepstool, she peered into the back of the safe. Fantastic! Just what she was looking for: a lockbox. And just as she'd hoped, it wasn't locked. "No need to double the security, eh, old man? It's already in a safe."

She rifled through manila envelopes. None of the labels interested her, nor were there any bearer bonds, cash, or jewels. She'd let the miscellaneous documents sit for a while. After she married into the family, she'd find out which were the most valuable. Right now, she needed something she could flip for fast cash. Something small that wouldn't be missed. Maybe some juicy blackmail material…

And there it was. A bundle of old letters, folded and without envelopes, tied with a skinny blue ribbon, a torn piece of paper slipped under the knot, the name Dan and an address hastily scrawled in pencil on it. On the reverse was 'Get map on Halloween from little man.'

The paper the letters were written on looked to be at least a hundred years old, brittle and yellowed. It didn't matter if these were two minutes or two hundred years old, though. It's what was written on them that was important. A family's reputation didn't have an expiration date. The right people would pay plenty to keep their name respectable, whether an affair of the heart was current or occurred two centuries earlier.

"Come to Mama, you sweet little love letters. Let's see what secrets you're hiding."

Clotilde picked at the tight ribbon, loosening the knot with her enameled fingernails. "Keep them in the same order, Lady C. Take only enough dirt to see you through until you're married and can access the big money. No need to be greedy."

"Got it!" After twenty minutes of squinting at the faded script, scanning the letters for bank account numbers or keywords such as 'my dearest,' 'love,' or 'I must have you,' she gave up. Or almost did. Her search had started at the back of the pile, thinking those would be the most current and contain the most valuable extortion information.

Nope.

Not only was the top one the easiest to read, but it was also the most intriguing. Still hard to make out without her reading glasses, it was as old as the others, written on the same splotchy paper. But this one was written in ballpoint pen! The ink was faded but consistent, not the blobs and faint streaks reminiscent of quill and ink. The penmanship was different, too: straightforward, a blocky, crisp print, not the twisty, flowery script of two hundred years ago.

She scanned for the easiest to read words. "You saw me only yesterday?" she read aloud. "Two hundred and thirty years?"

She set the letter under the bright desk lamp and squinted at the words.

Dear James,

I know it seems like you saw me only yesterday, but if all has gone according to instructions, you will be getting this 230 years after I have written it. I think you can verify this if you have the paper dated. Remember that strange man, Simon? He does have something to do with us, or rather me. I followed him into the park, and I accidentally fell through time. Right now, I am living with your ancestors. I actually married your great – I don't know how many times over – uncle's son. I think I found the Revolutionary War relative you were looking for. That is, if you were looking for Lord Julian Wallace Hart, brother of Lord Anthony Melbourne. Julian's a wonderful man, and his (step) son and I have three children (triplets!).

The reason for my letter is that I want you to contact my daughter, Leah Madigan. Please, share this:
Leah,

I am alive and well in 1781. All the stories by Lisa Sinclaire are pretty much true. I will show up again on August 4, 2013 at the hospital you work in, but you will have to let me return home to my new family. You are bright and grown up now, and can live life on your own, but my babies and my new husband, Wallace Pomeroy-Hart, need me. Sarah and Jody Pomeroy are as wonderful as you told me and as the history (not science fiction or fantasy) books say. It is possible to change history on a small scale or I wouldn't be here with your siblings who are nearly 200 years older than you.

James, as of August 4, 2013, Leah is working at the Moses H. Cone Memorial Hospital in Greensboro, not far from our little cafe. She was, will be, my recovery room nurse. So, if you have a chance to talk to her in person, would you please explain what happened and let her read this letter? I love her very much and don't want her to worry about me. Oh, and I have a new first name: Evie. I'll write more as time goes by, but please do not read any other letters (I hope to get a journal started for you/her) until you get a chance to speak with her and let this settle in for both of you.

Hugs and kisses from me and your great-many-times-over uncles and love from, Mom

"What in the hell?" Clotilde huffed. "Talk about a scam. Looks like the old man is trying to run some big-time con." She

7

chuckled and shook her head, a new respect dawning for the silver fox. "James, it looks like your grandfather is a first-class con artist."

Or was he? She fingered the paper and broke off a corner that didn't have writing on it. It crumpled it into dust. "It sure feels old, but how'd he get the ink to fade? Set it in the sun for a year or two?" She bent over the first letter again and sniffed. "Strange. It smells herbal." She scratched a dark gray bump in the paper and inhaled again. "Lavender. Handmade paper with flowers in it."

She pushed the pile of letters away, not sure whether she was disgusted or intrigued. "Why would these be in a safe? Either Marty's scamming someone or there really is a time traveler out there trying to reconnect with her daughter. So, who is this Mom person? Pbbt! Time travel is the con. A lost mommy is just the hook, something to get the bleeding-heart suckers interested."

Clotilde grabbed the scrap of paper with the faded one-word name and address and squinted at it again. Her head was throbbing from reading without glasses, the words bouncing and skittering across the page. She had to figure out how to make money out of this letter – or letters – though.

Marty was out of the country. No way could she extort so much as a trinket out of him. Most likely, this Dan was in on the ruse with Marty and had the details on the gambit. She could do something with that. A few phone calls and she could have feet on the ground in the USA. A big, burly intimidator to get in this Dan's face should work. A broken leg or two and he'd be ready to give up the goods.

"Since I can't bleed the old man, I'll find someone here in London who wants to bury this. I'll bet the right person would pay a lot to keep it quiet that a member of the House of Lords is putting out forgeries and promoting fairy tales about time travel. They don't need another scandal or nut job in the House."

Buzz!

She looked down at her alert. Damn! Her hair appointment was in less than an hour and she still had to put everything back the way it was. She couldn't be late for Jean Pierre or he'd never see her again. And she wouldn't be seen at this weekend's gala with hair colored and coifed by anyone but him.

Clotilde copied the name and address from the little scrap of paper onto a sticky note. She remembered a keyword – an event – she'd seen on one of the other letters. She picked up the pile and scanned them. Aha! There it was.

Halloween.

A greedy American tradition marked by masks and extortion. She could get behind that. She read further. "So, Simon is a short man and they're to meet him on Halloween in Greensboro. James is to get the little guy's map somehow."

She wrote small, squeezing as much pertinent information onto the little yellow paper as she could. "Greensboro. Halloween. Map. Simon is little man. Damn! My pen ran out of ink." She looked at the date in the letter again. "2013? That's two years from now. Shit! What kind of hocus pocus is he trying to pull off? Crap. I need a drink. This sure as hell doesn't make any sense sober."

Frazzled and frantic, she hastily retied the bundle of letters and stuffed them in the lockbox. "Damn!" she broke a nail shoving the golden picture frame back in place but managed to get the room back into what she hoped was the right order.

"A facial, a couple of champagne cocktails, and maybe a little slap and tickle with Randy before James picks me up for dinner. He'll be glad I'm happy. He just doesn't have to know why."

***

The next afternoon

"Ah, Maurice," Clotilde said, her hand out for her favorite shady town contact.

He kissed the air above her knuckles, hoping to keep the smell of her acrid perfume out of his nose and off his mustache. If he didn't, he'd be breathing her stink for hours. "And how may I assist you?"

"Give me your phone," she said.

"Excuse me?" he asked but handed it over.

She fumbled with it, found the camera icon, and snapped a photo of her note with the copied address from the bundle of letters. She held up her image to him. "Do you have a contact in this part of America? I have a little…" Clotilde bit her bottom lip seductively, hoping to get a better rate from the boss of the underworld employment agency.

"Intimidation?" he asked.

"Yes, that's what it is. I just want to garner someone's attention. And get a little information, too."

"And if you happen to get a few quid at the same time?" Maurice asked, one eyebrow raised, the other winking.

"I always knew you were the smartest crook," she said, petting his arm and 'oohing' at his powerful muscle.

Instead of flattering him, though, she had disgusted him even further. No one called Maurice a crook and got away with it.

The powerful man stretched his mustache ear to ear in hatred masked as delight. "I have just the pair for you. They always work together. But hey, I don't want to take away any of your *profit*, so I'll just give you their contact info. You can reach out to them yourself and cut out the middleman."

Maurice pulled a burner phone out of his coat pocket. He typed in 'America' then brought out his own phone to verify the number. He held his broad hand out flat, offering it to her. "Your phone, *mademoiselle*."

Clotilde scowled at his insistence before remembering to put on her gracious face. No need to waste seduction on him. He'd already agreed to a freebie. "Thank you," she said, smiling sweetly. She picked it up with thumb and one finger, pinkie extended as if disposing of a soiled nappy.

"Just give them a call. They're known as Vinnie and Hugo. They're reasonably priced, too. Just don't pay them the full amount before the deed is done. Americans are so irresponsible at times, but they do enjoy their work. You'll get what you deserve, I'm sure."

Suddenly, Maurice patted the pocket of his custom-made leather jacket. "Excuse me. I have to take this call," he said, pretending it had just vibrated an alert. The big man nodded in farewell and turned away from her, holding back his smirk of deception.

"Just what you deserve, for sure," he said softly into the phone with no one on the other end. "Dumb and Dumber are always finding new ways to screw up. I'm sure they'll mess up whatever you have for them, too."

Chapter 2: Change of Venue

August 2011
Tempe, Arizona

He held her in his arms, the tremble of her shivers shooting through the thin fabric of her scanty shift to his callused hands like a fistful of pebbles on a pond. He wrapped his plaid higher around her shoulders, trying to protect her from the wind and rain. "Ye'll be safe with me as long as I'm near, Sass..."

"Don't...don't call me that," Sarah stammered as she shrugged out from under him and into the downpour. "I'm not a slut."

"That jest means yer a foreigner, not from around here," Jody explained, holding the gray and brown fabric open as an invitation for her to come back to its warmth. "I meant no disrespect."

After a moment's hesitation, she nodded, acknowledging him with a hint of a smile "I...I knew – or at least, I suspected – that's what it meant." She gulped in a damp breath of courage, eager to snuggle back into his muscular body's heat, grateful for his nearness. Despite only knowing him for a few hours, she felt comfortable with him. She was still leery of being so close to any man who wasn't her spouse, though, especially in a region – or time – whose customs were foreign to her.

She pulled back her shoulders, resolute, and looked him in the eye. "As I said before, my name is Sarah. You haven't known me long enough to give me a pet name."

"A pet?" The big Scot grinned wryly and shook his head. "Yer no dog, but I'll do as ye ask." He paused and added, "Sarah." He waved his plaid gently, a silent admonition to come share the warmth.

"Thank you," she said and squirmed close, ready for every fraction of a degree of heat he had to offer.

Oops. The accidental time traveler discretely shifted her position. Either her nearness or her wriggling – or both – had excited him. His conversation was casual, but his true feelings toward her were punctuated by his rigid male member. Certainly, he was aware of the change in his anatomy. How could he not be? Thankfully, nothing on her body would show she was getting aroused. And she certainly wasn't going to tell him she felt the same way!

This instant attraction she felt toward him, whether solely from friction or gratitude, was wrong. So very wrong. It shouldn't be happening. She was a married woman. Or was she? Her husband – or even his father's father's father – hadn't been born yet!'

Leah put the Sprawl-Mart sales receipt bookmark in the paperback and set it on the bedstand. It was late. She had covered four extra hours for her shift relief at the hospital. The poor gal had called in late, saying her obstetrician's appointments were backed up. She couldn't be seen for three more hours; could Leah cover for her?

"At least it's not me with a bun in the oven," Leah said aloud. "Poor girl."

She switched off the light, fluffed her pillow, then tried to relax her shoulders, hoping sleep would follow soon.

Who was she trying to kid? She envied the woman.

Leah never bragged about how much she enjoyed her independence. That would be a slap in the face to the two newlywed and one very pregnant members of her crew. She was both happy and relieved that she had an uncomplicated life, though. It would be a simple matter to pack up a few boxes and leave if the whim hit.

And it had.

"Just one more week, and you'll be away from Arizona," she crowed to the near empty apartment. "North Carolina, here I come."

***

"You never did say why you were leaving," the administrator said, prompting for an answer to a question she legally wasn't supposed to ask.

Leah rolled her eyes. This was her first exit interview. 'Don't burn bridges,' her mother had told her. 'You might need to come back.'

Not *want* to come back but *need* to come back. Yeah, right, Mom. You never did have faith in me, did you?

"Ahem," Ms. Jones cleared her throat.

"Sorry," Leah apologized meekly. "Just choosing my words. Actually, this is a fine place to work. The facility is top-notch, and I get along great with my co-workers. I don't have one complaint. The one thing you're not able to change, though, is the outside environment. I've had enough of Arizona. I think I'd like to live in an area of the country where I don't have to deal with six months of temperatures over a hundred degrees and at least that many months of dealing with allergies."

Ms. Jones had just grabbed a tissue as Leah finished her short dissertation. "I hear that one," she said, dabbing her dribbly nose. "I've only been here four years and I'm already looking for a hay fever-free zone. Let me know if you find one."

"Will do."

"Um, I'm not supposed to ask, and this isn't going into any records, but where are you going? I'm asking for me, not the hospital."

"Greensboro, North Carolina," Leah said, chin out with pride.

"Oh, isn't that in the area *Lost* was supposed to take place? Oh, maybe you haven't read that book…" Ms. Jones added, a blush rising.

14

"Are you kidding?" Leah chuckled. "Yeah, don't tell anyone, but that's the number one reason I chose that part of the world. I know Jody and Sarah Pomeroy are fictional, but I'd still like to check out the area where they could have lived. That is, if time travel was real. Can you imagine?"

"Imagine? Oh, yeah," Ms. Jones crooned, a wide smile rising. "If you find anything promising, let me know. I may not make the move there, but that doesn't mean I won't take a week of my vacation to check it out. Wouldn't that be weird if time travel was real and there really was a Jody Pomeroy? Maybe I could get back there before Sarah…"

"Geez, Marjorie," Leah said, "you have it worse than I do."

"Yeah, well, I guess it's possible someone loves that series more than me," she said, then winked. "But I don't think so."

Ms. Jones checked a box on the bottom of the form in front of her and signed her name. She turned it around and pushed it toward Leah. "You're available for rehire if you decide to come back. Just sign here that we spoke and that you have no issues with the hospital or its agents."

As Leah was signing, Marjorie grabbed one of her business cards, flipped it over, and scribbled a quick note. "And here's my home phone number and email address. Let's keep in touch. I am so going to live vicariously through you."

"I'll do that," Leah said, then stood up. She reached out to shake hands. "That is, of course, until you move east and can explore it for yourself."

"I might just do that."

***

"Already? I thought you weren't leaving until next spring."

Leah put the phone on speaker mode and set it down, continuing her tasks. "Mom, the job I found wants me right away," she said. "Besides, I just have a few totes of personal stuff. I never felt comfortable buying furniture for a place that I might want to walk away from."

"Well, you got that one right," Dani said, then stifled a groan. *I hope I didn't say something wrong. Again.*

Leah changed her subtle growl of anger into an exaggerated throat clearing, adding a slight cough at the end. *Are you saying I always get everything else wrong?* She channeled her rage into energy, hoisting the tote of books onto the counter.

"I'm not taking all my books," she said, starting a new and neutral topic of conversation. "Just the ones I can't live without. I have loads of duplicates." She grabbed an empty box and started transferring some of the hardcover books into a new container, setting the others off to the side.

"I'll send you some of those. I'm packing clothes and sundries on top of my books so none of the boxes are too heavy. Any you don't want, you can donate to the library in Fairbanks or wherever."

"Don't you think they have enough books already?" her mother asked.

"Probably, but they also use them for fundraising events. Public libraries sell outdated, surplus, or duplicate books to raise money to buy new ones they don't have. Everybody wins. Oh, here. I'm putting a rubber band around one I want you to keep. You really need to read it. It's my favorite book ever. It's sort of a late Christmas gift. I meant to buy you a new copy but never was at the right place when I remembered."

Leah set her least dog-eared paperback version of *Lost* on top of the stack of books. "You really ought to read it someday. It's about the most perfect man in the world. Maybe you won't be so soured on men after you check out Jody Pomeroy."

"Isn't that the time travel romance everyone's raving over? The one by Lisa Sinclaire?"

"Yup, that's the one. You should read it just so you know what they're talking about," Leah said as she went back to packing kitchen items, letting her mother either continue or wrap up their semi-annual phone call.

"Lisa Sinclaire." Dani paused, then said, "Hmm. Her name is like mine."

"Huh?" Leah asked, setting the newspaper-wrapped glass coffee pot on the counter.

"Her first name is mixed up in her last name. You know," she said. "Look at it. All the letters of Lisa are in Sinclaire. And all the letters of Dani are in Madigan. Our names are the same but different."

"If you say so…" Leah said, brusquely grabbing another sheet of newspaper to wrap the rest of the coffee maker. "Hey, I gotta cut this short. I only have a few more hours, and then I'm outta here. I told the landlord he could have it back by five."

"Oh, I'm sorry. Bad timing on my part, I guess," she said, her voice trying to be bright but her last two words betraying her perpetual insecurity. "Drive safely and give me a call when you get there. Or in a day or two. Whenever it's convenient. I mean…"

Leah heard her mother's unease and grimaced as she cut in. "How about I call you within twenty-four hours of getting there?"

"Sounds good to me. Take care out there. Love you."

"Love you, too, Mom." Leah ended the call and put the phone back on the counter. She exhaled deeply, frustrated but relieved the call was over. "But I'm sure glad you're far away in Alaska and not here trying to micromanage me."

Leah grumbled as she picked up more packing paper. "Who are you trying to fool, woman? Her worrying about you is not the same as trying to control you. If you had a daughter, you'd worry about her, too. Cut her some slack."

Leah looked up at the laminated photo still stuck to the refrigerator with an Arizona Diamondbacks magnet. Her

17

kindergarten graduation picture, Mom and Dad on either side of her as she held up her construction-paper framed diploma. "Yeah, we were a happy family for a while. At least I still have memories and photographs. I guess that's more than some people have."

Chapter 3: Immense Insecurities

Fairbanks, Alaska
August 20, 2010

"Well, that went over like a fajita fart at a funeral service," Dani said, hanging up the phone. "When will I ever learn? Write, don't call. You can't delete words after you say them like you can before sending an email. Damn it! Damn! Damn! Damn!"

She kissed the back of her fist, tender from where she'd punctuated her curses on the coffee table. She looked around and snorted as she realized she didn't have anyone in her life – even a pet – to frighten with her outburst. "If a parent falls and there's no one to hear her, is she really hurt?"

Ding!

"Saved from Self-pity Philosophy 101 by the bell. Dinner for one, coming up."

Clutching the arms of her recliner, the sixty-year-old overweight divorcée leaned forward and stood up. "Well, I guess it's a good thing I didn't have more kids. At least I can only disappoint one child."

Taking the cookie sheet out of the oven, she grimaced at the stench emanating from the foil pan filled with broccoli-topped salmon. "Really? I'm supposed to enjoy this crap? Maybe I could if it was covered with a thick buttery sauce and preceded by a magnum of wine. And with the promise of a dessert of deep-dish apple crisp with vanilla ice cream."

The 'eating program' book her doctor had suggested said that presentation was very important in enjoying a meal, as was dressing for the occasion. So, before preparing the fish and vegetables, she had set the table with real linen and china. No paper towels and pressed fiber disposable plates tonight. Now it was time to play dress up for a fine *haute cuisine* dinner eaten in, even if it was so lame she couldn't even conjure up a fantasy guy to sit with her.

Dani thumbed through the clothes hanging in her closet and found her favorite poofy blouse and nice pair of black slacks she hadn't worn in years. She threw the outfit on the bed and decided to check the size of the pants before scooting out of her comfy gray sweatpants. "Oh, hell no," she said. "I'll never fit a size twelve again. At least, not in this lifetime."

She returned the blouse to the closet, then took the pants off the hanger, folded them neatly, and set them aside. "I'll purge the closet of skinny-lady clothes after dinner. Or tomorrow. Sometime later. Right now, if I'm gonna eat grizzly bear food, I want to be comfortable doing it."

Two bites into the overcooked salmon and singed broccoli casserole, Dani pushed her plate away. "Next time I try this crap, I'll put it on a paper plate. At least then I can throw the whole works away at the same time. Now I have to smell it while I'm washing the dishes, too."

She stood up from the table, disgusted. "Plus, it's too stinky for a garbage disposal." She scraped the uneaten fare on top of the rest of the pink and green concoction still in the disposable aluminum pan, then folded the works over into a mass and tossed it into the kitchen trash. She pulled the tie closure on the bag, secured it, then set it in the outdoor garbage can. "Good riddance. Anyhow, eating salmon makes bears fat, so I think I'll pass."

While washing her hands, Dani remembered she still had a few apples left plus a cabinet full of staples. A grin spread across her face. And she had cream for her coffee. A little flour, fat, and salt and she could make a pie crust. Sliced apples, cinnamon, and sugar would make a fast pie filling. And while it was baking, she could whip the cream with a sprinkle of powdered sugar for a sweet topping that was as good as – if not better than – vanilla ice cream.

"Yeah, yeah. I'm my own worst enemy when it comes to eating right. But I'd rather be plump and happy than skinny and so bitchy that nobody – not even mosquitoes – would get near me." She frowned. "Well, I think mosquitoes will go for anyone. I doubt there's enough money in Alaska to pay someone to be my friend if I had to live on fish and greens. I am who I am, so live with that or leave me alone."

***

Later

Half an apple pie and two cups of whipped cream later, Dani fell into a 'sugar coma' on the couch. Sated but not sick.

Dreams came, bright and vibrant. She was young again. Healthy, full of energy, devoid of pain, she was running and leaping without abandon, unencumbered by the stresses of deadlines and responsibilities. She was in a forest. Not an Alaskan one, but one lush with gray-green beards of mossy growth hanging from the branches. Velvet waistcoats of bright green ivy hugged tree trunks with a friendly embrace, fallen acorn mast and golden leaves carpeted the verdant forest floor. Scotland? Or Appalachia, maybe?

Little creases wrinkled the sleeper's eyes and her lips spread wide. Even unconscious, she felt her smile blossoming, a pure joy and happiness she seldom experienced when awake. Dani sighed deeply and shifted positions, relaxing into the embrace of bliss. Her back twinged at the movement on the uncomfortable couch. The spasm of excruciating pain jerked her out of her sweet slumber and tossed her into a sudden rage.

"Crap, crap, crap!" she huffed. Instinct kicked in and after a few moments of slow deep breathing, the pang lessened into a gnawing ache, allowing her to sit up. "Damn! How can I get that dream back?"

She looked over at the bottle of wine she had received from a client for Christmas eight months ago, then up at the clock above the kitchen window. "Six-thirty already? Too early to start drinking, even if I did indulge. Probably wouldn't bring back that youthful feeling, anyhow. It's not too early for a shower and a pot of Columbia's finest, though."

Brring! Brring!

"Who could be calling this early? Hello?"

Dani waited until the caller took a breath from his sales spiel, then let him have it at full volume. "I understand you have quotas to fill, but anyone who doesn't have enough sense to know that Alaska is four hours *earlier* than east coast time will never get my business. Please put me on your do not call list."

"But...but... I'm sorry. If you just give me a ..."

Click!

"You had your chance to schedule your calls when you got to work."

Brring! Brring!

She looked at the out of state number on the caller ID. "Not another one!" she growled, then picked up the phone and barked, "Yeah? Don't you know what time it is in Alaska?"

"Um... I was calling to see if Audie Madigan is available," a timid male asked.

"Huh? I mean, no, she's not. Who's calling and why?" she asked, switching to her amiable professional voice.

"This is the emergency contact number she put on her job application. We were expecting her this morning and she didn't show up."

"Wait. What? Is this that hospital in North Carolina?" Dani asked, sitting down at the kitchen table, scared, shocked, and confused.

"Yes, ma'am. I'm with the human resources department at Moses H. Cone Hospital."

22

"Oh, shit. I mean, shoot. Leah said she didn't have to be there for a week. She left Arizona yesterday. She figured it wouldn't take more than three days to get there."

"Leah? I'm sorry. I must have the wrong number."

"Wait! No, that's her middle name – what family calls her. Audie is her first name. Are you sure about the date? She said she didn't have to be there until August 27th."

Dani heard the clack, clack of a keyboard and shuffling of papers. "Oh, I'm so sorry to have disturbed you. Yes, it was sloppy handwriting on this end. I thought she was supposed to be here the twenty-first, but you're right; it's the twenty-seventh. Please ignore the call. Have a good day." *Click.*

Hands fumbling, Dani set the phone on the table. "Well, that sure got my heart going." She looked up at the calendar again. "Shoot. Monday, trash day. I'd better get that can to the curb. I don't want fish and broccoli marinating outside my backdoor for a week."

She pushed the start button on the coffee pot, slipped on her Crocs, held her breath in case the stench had escaped the can, then stepped outside. She rolled the refuse container with a week's worth of garbage and her failed dinner out of the shelter of her apartment porch to the sidewalk's edge. Two steps later, she took a deep breath of untainted air, grateful the prevailing breeze was blowing the stink of old fish and singed greens downwind. "Compost in peace," she said under her breath and walked back toward her apartment unit.

Huff. Huff. Huff.

Startled, Dani looked up at the strange yet familiar noise. "Oh, no! Not again!" She ran to the first parked car in the lot and used its bulk as a barrier between her and the angry mother moose with a calf in tow. She hadn't noticed her when she came out, then realized she should have been on the lookout. The trees were freckled with newly blushed crabapples, practically calling out to

23

the oversized ungulates in the neighborhood. Plus, last week, her new – and very ignorant – neighbor tried on more than one occasion to entice a big brown cow and her two calves with carrots to get them closer for a photo shoot.

The mama moose moved toward Dani with slow deliberate steps, her head down, ready to prove dominance.

"Hey, I didn't do anything wrong," Dani said, moving from the front of the parked pickup to the dented side of its bed for more protection. "Shoot, I don't even eat moose meat."

The cow huffed again then stopped, lifted its head, and looked behind – not at – her.

"Sorry. I guess that was rude," she babbled, then realized the moose had changed focus and was no longer looking at her, but at something behind her. Dani pivoted in place, making sure the truck was still between her and the unpredictable wildlife. "What's the matter?"

When she sidestepped to the back of the old F250, she saw it. The young moose's twin was tangled in the bird netting wrapped around the neighbor's crabapple tree.

"Oh, please find a way out," Dani chanted as the three-month-old moose kicked and twisted frantically in the dark-green nylon. "Please, please do it by yourself."

"Stay put," a stern female voice called out from the side yard.

Dani looked up and saw her new neighbor approach the netted calf with a set of shears. She looked back at the mother moose who was huffing and snorting again but now had her ears back, ready to charge. "Make it quick then get back in the house," Dani ordered. "And no pictures!"

Too close to get a running start at a gallop, the mother moose took ten determined steps to her estranged baby, the other calf following behind her.

Snip! Snip! Snip! "He's free," the daring neighbor shouted as she dashed inside, slamming the front door behind her. She pulled her window open and hollered out, "And no more carrots or snacks for them, either. I didn't realize moose were so big!"

Dani scrambled toward her own apartment, pausing just long enough to look back and shout, "Good idea," behind her.

"Whoa, there," a stout and burly dark-haired man said, one hand up to keep her from falling over.

Dani stumbled away from the up-close encounter, her face red at the full-on body slam. "Who? What? I mean, may I help you?"

The man snorted in derision. "I was looking for Dan Madigan. I hear he makes some awesome websites."

"That's *Dani* Madigan, and you're correct except for one major difference. He's a she. Oh, and the she is me."

Another snort of disdain escaped as the man reached into his front pants pocket. He pulled out a torn piece of notebook paper with pencil scribbles on it. "I don't think so. It says Dan and Dan is a man's name."

"Well, I don't know how you got this address. I do all my business over the phone or via email," Dani said, pulling her unbuttoned flannel shirt closer with one hand and thumbing her fallen hair behind one ear with the other. When he didn't respond, she looked at him with narrowed eyes, letting him know she wasn't about to be bullied by his size or belief that his hasty note was correct. She looked at her watch. "And during regular business hours."

"Hmph." He looked at his note again, then glared at her.

"I don't care what that says," she insisted, shoulders back. "Way Fine Websites is my business and I *do not* have a public office. If you care to discuss web designs and hosting, you can call or email me."

"Since I'm already here, let me look at what you got. I'll see if you're as good as this Dan fella is supposed to be."

Now it was Dani's turn to show disfavor. She turned her back on him and shook her head in disgust. "Men," she snorted and started to leave.

A heavy hand on her shoulder stopped her with a firm grasp. "No woman walks away from me," he growled.

"Is there a problem here?" a man's voice called out from nearby.

Dani looked up and saw a tall but slightly built red-haired man walk out from the shadows of the building.

The once-aggressive brute slowly removed his hand, not wanting to acknowledge he had done anything wrong. "Just a mistaken identity, I guess," he said to the newcomer, then turned his attention back to the older woman and curled his upper lip in a silent snarl.

She replied wordlessly, her chin pointed at him as if it were a knife to his throat.

The hefty mugger growled, "Tell your boss, *Dan*, that I'll be in touch about that web stuff I need. Tell him I'll make it worth his while."

Dark eyes focused forward and face frozen in a scowl, the big man left, crowding the pathway so Dani's interloping savior – a much lighter man – had to step off the sidewalk or be walked over.

As soon as he was out of sight, Dani walked over to the redhead and said, "I don't know who you are, but thanks."

"My duty, honor, and privilege."

"Huh?" she asked, squinting in confusion.

He leaned forward slightly, not close enough to invade her personal space but letting her know he had a secret to share.

She leaned toward him. "What?"

"I'm a cop," he said softly, then stood up straight, grinning. "I was checking out this place as a rental. I decided to do a walk around on my way to work. They listed a couple of vacancies last week and I wanted to see if any were still available."

"It's down to one," Dani said. "I just got a new neighbor a few days ago." She frowned. "Are you Alaskan?"

"Pretty much. Not born here, but I've been around a while. Why? Does it make a difference?" he asked, his inquiring detective mind not suggesting an answer but still feeling a slight.

"Moose," Dani said. "The new lady was feeding the mama moose who's been coming around the neighborhood, snacking on crabapples. I know she's been trying for a few good photos – the woman, not the moose. As I'm sure you know, once you feed them, they keep coming back, wanting more. That brazen cow just about knocked me down a few minutes ago." She shuddered and clarified. "The moose, not the neighbor."

He chuckled. "Don't worry about me. Moose belong in the wild. It's mostly the fruit-filled trees and ornamentals that draw them into town or they'd stay away," he said.

"Especially the tulips," she added. "Oh, I'm Dani Madigan. I live right there. And just for the record, I'd feel more secure if you did move into the complex. Not that I'm needy, but I am sixty, single, and work from home. That masher gave me the creeps."

Dani reached around herself and grabbed her elbows, shivering as the realization hit her. "I...I don't know what would have happened if you hadn't shown up."

The detective set his hand on her shoulder. "You were doing fine standing your ground when I saw you. I just wanted to make sure he didn't push it. Bullies don't like to be challenged. Oh, and I'm Arlie Biggar," he said, handing her a business card. "Any problems with the apartment units that the landlord wouldn't divulge?"

"No. There's covered parking and he's good about keeping the snow plowed in the winter. You have to pay utilities, but that's pretty much standard everywhere now. It has gas heat, a decent-sized kitchen, and lots of south-facing windows. You have to use

27

blackout curtains in the summer, but I sure love having at least a little bit of natural light in winter."

"Ah, the abundance of sunshine in the summer and lack of it in the winter. I'm from Anchorage where the daylight hours aren't quite as extreme as here in Fairbanks."

"Well, I have the landlord's phone number upstairs if you need it," Dani said. "I sure hope you like this place. As I said, I'd feel more comfortable if you were around."

"I'll pop in and say hi if I move in. Or should I call or email you?" he asked with a wink.

"For you, pop in is fine. I already told you where I live. Besides, how could you phone or email me? I didn't give you my contact info." she asked, grinning.

"I heard you say your business was called Way Fine Websites. Public information for anyone who wants to look, I'm sure."

She shook her head and laughed. "Well, you did say you were a cop. A detective, maybe? I hope to see you around."

He nodded. "And I'll see if I can find out anything about the man who was just here. His van had his company name on it. He's probably legit, but a minute or two checking him out would make both of us feel more secure."

"Yes, it would. Thank you," Dani said, waving goodbye before her delayed tears of fear sprang free.

***

"Hey, Vinnie, what'd you find out about that computer nerd? Did he look like an easy target?" Hugo asked as he mined another blob of wax from his ear with a paperclip.

Vinnie grumbled as he jerked open the passenger door of the stolen metallic-red van. "Just shut up and drive for a minute. There's a nosy punk hanging around here. He stopped me from finding out where this Dan guy is."

28

The former heavyweight contender sat down, then reached over and grabbed the mega-size soda in the cupholder. He took a long drink, ending with a loud slurp that indicated he'd emptied it.

"Hey, that was mine," Hugo said.

"Yeah, well I was the one doing all the work. Let's get back on the road and score a couple more. Plus, I have a bone to pick with you and I don't want no one eavesdropping. Seems like you take lousy notes."

"Hey, I told you when Clotilde called that I didn't want to talk to her. I can't understand that limey accent of hers. Besides, I think she's kinda sweet on you, Vinnie."

Vinnie grinned and settled into his seat, enjoying the praise, then realized that even though Hugo was dim, he still knew how to manipulate people, including him. "How could she be sweet on me? She's never seen me."

"Maybe she heard you were a world-famous boxer or something and looked you up," Hugo said, looking away as he lied.

"Nah, doesn't matter. I wouldn't have nuthin' to do with someone that lives that far away. She'd probably want me to change jobs or work for free." Vinnie pulled the crumpled note out of his pocket.

"Speakin' of jobs, your note says 'Get rid of Dan Madagun, webstate dee-ziner.' I figured out the last part. There's no zee in designer, by the way. And I could see how Madigan sounds like Madagun, but are you sure she said Dan and not Danielle?"

Hugo spotted a fast-food drive through and made a quick left, throwing Vinnie off balance and practically into his lap. "Oops. Sorry," he said as his brother and partner in crime for the last five years pulled himself together.

"Well?"

"Oh, yeah. Dan or Danny or Daniel: they're all the same, right? I mean, I was runnin' out of room on that paper so *pre-reviated* it."

29

"The word's *abbreviated*, imbecile."

Hugo stomped on the brakes, sending Vinnie flying again, this time into the windshield. "I told you, don't call me names like that!"

Vinnie quickly rubbed his forehead to check for blood, then pushed on the dashboard and got situated again. "Yeah, you're right. That was rude." He reached around and grabbed the seatbelt, buckling it across his chest. "I guess wearing this wouldn't be such a bad idea today. My horoscope said to watch out for the unexpected. Now, you're sure that Lady Clotilde person said we were looking for a guy named Dan or Danny or Daniel? Could she have said it was a woman and you forgot to write that down?"

"Hold on a sec," Hugo said, his hand up. He rolled his window down and said, "Two big colas – but not the colossal size because those don't fit in the cup holders – a super-big order of fries, an order of onion rings, and two apple pies." He turned to Vinnie. "Did you want something, too?"

"Yeah, get me a cola, a big order of fries, and a supersized chocolate malt." Vinnie rolled his window down and threw Hugo's empty cup out the window. "And you're buying this time."

Two minutes, a wink to the tattooed teenage server, and a ten-dollar tip later, the dim-witted duo was back on the road to their hotel room by the Chena River.

"I still say she said, 'Just get rid of this Danny character," Hugo said as he settled onto one of the two queen-sized beds in the suite.

"Just the name, no information about gender?" Vinnie asked.

"Genitals?"

"No, Hugo. Gender, not genitals. They both have to do with sex, but they're not the same word."

"I didn't know we were gonna get to have sex on this job. But you know me pretty good, Vinnie. I don't do guys."

Vinnie shook his head, too tired to argue. He pulled the note out of his pocket and handed it to Hugo. "Read this to me, okay?"

"I thought you could read. What's wrong? Got somethin' in your eye?"

"No." He shook the paper at Hugo. "Just maybe I didn't understand what you wrote."

Hugo took the crumpled notebook paper and spread it out on the top of the end table. He squinted at it, then turned on the light. "Oh, yeah. It's kinda hard to read in pencil, huh?"

"Yeah. Just read it."

"'Take out Dan at Way Fine…something or other.' I can't read my own writing. I think it says webstates. And then there's the address. I got that part right, didn't I?" Hugo asked with pride.

"Yeah, you did. And the word is websites, not web-states. Are you sure she said Dan, not Danny?"

Hugo shrugged, then picked up the laminated folder near the lamp. "Maybe. I don't write too fast. Hey, look here. They have room service." He ran his finger down the list. "I could do with a couple orders of deep-fried shrimp."

"You just ate!"

"Yeah, well I had the chips. Now it's time for the fish. Only I like shrimp better. I sure hope that credit card hasn't been called in as stolen yet."

"Don't worry," Vinnie said, pulling out a rubber-band secured bundle. "I have about twenty more fresh ones."

Hugo looked up and grinned at their deck of financial security cards. "So, what are we gonna do about that Dan woman?"

"I'll give it a few hours, then call Clotilde and ask her to describe the hit. Oh, and you're right. A big plate of shrimp with extra cocktail sauce sounds good. Here's hoping they'll deliver booze to the room, too. Otherwise, you'll have to make a beer run."

31

Chapter 4: First Day at Work

August 27, 2010
Greensboro, North Carolina

The brisk evening breeze blew through Sarah's hair, lifting her dark curly locks away from her eyes. Hopefully, it would dry her tears before Jody could see them overflow to paint shiny lines down her cheeks. How could she tell him she was leaving, back to her own time, her home, her career... and her husband.

Watching his broad chest rise and fall in deep slumber, she reached out, ready to touch his leg in farewell, then realized she didn't want him to wake.

They'd barely spoken to one another in the last two days. Her unabating anger at him for embarrassing her in front of his kinsmen was hard to forgive. Why couldn't men of this time realize a woman had a voice, too? That her opinion counted. Or should.

Besides, if he awoke, there was the real possibility of make-up sex. She'd enjoy it too much. She always did. He was a thorough lover, satisfying her needs whether he was tender and compassionate or rutting like an elk in season. If they joined again, she might not be able to find the nerve to leave.

"Is something amiss, Sass...Sarah?" he stammered, almost slipping and calling her the name he only uttered in the throes of passion.

Sarah sniffed and wiped a lock of non-existent hair out of her eyes, blotting away an escaped tear with the back of her hand. "Don't worry about it. If that's what you call all your women, go ahead and call me that. After all, from what I understand, you and your kin think all women are alike. You only use given names, so you don't double-claim the same one."

"Nae. That isna true," Jody said. "It's the sire who names the lass – or laddie – when the bairn is born."

"Why? Because the mother, the woman who carried the child and will be solely responsible for its health and feeding for at least two years, isn't smart enough to choose a name? She's just a brood creature or less. Just a warm spot for a man to stick his..."

Leah slammed the paperback book closed and stuck in the slip of hair ribbon she'd been using as her favorite bookmark since high school. "I know what comes next and I don't want to get all wound up before starting my first day at work." She checked the time on the clock, reached over, and clicked off the alarm before it rang.

"Ready or not, here I come."

This was Leah's fourth day in her new apartment in Greensboro. The first day she'd spent unpacking the few boxes she'd brought with her. The next day, she bought groceries and sundry household items she didn't want to bring across country. The third day was reserved for R and R: recuperating and reading. Fully recharged, she was now both ready and eager to tackle her scheduled three consecutive twelve-hour workdays at her new hospital.

What she wasn't keen on was the ominous task of remembering everyone's name and learning the workplace pecking order. Name tags with job positions would help – unless they were on a hangtag and twisted backward – but it was her co-workers' *real* functions and status she needed to discover and memorize. Who was the sharpest on the floor when dealing with an emergency? Who was best connected for dealing with other departments? Who was golden when you wanted to swap shifts for stacking days off for a mini vacation?

She looked at the clock for the tenth time in as many minutes, then at the coffee pot with just a stain of java left in it. Still thirty minutes before she had to leave for work. "Oh, what the hell? Might as well find out what cafeteria caffeine tastes like."

33

Not one of the eight hospital-green clad employees turned to see who the tangle-footed person was who had just stumbled into the dining room. Even those who had worked at the hospital for ten years regularly tripped over the aluminum threshold transition between the hall and eating area. All their attention was sucked up by reading the morning news and emails on their phones.

"Um, am I supposed to pay for the coffee somewhere?" Leah asked, noticing no one was at the register and the only food was an opened pink box of mixed bagels and donuts.

A blonde woman looked up and smiled. "Nah, this time of day the coffee is free. We take turns bringing in finger foods for breakfast. Today was my treat. I'm lazy, so we're having drive-through junk food. You'd better go ahead and grab a bite. That coffee might burn a hole in your gut if you drink it on an empty stomach. It's almost as strong as carbolic acid when KK makes it."

"Thanks for the warning," Leah said. She poured half a cup, then grabbed two plastic containers of creamer and a cinnamon sugar cruller.

"Go ahead and sit here," the woman said. "You must be Audie. I saw on the schedule we were finally getting help."

Leah forgot the name tag the human resources woman had given her had her legal first name, not the one she normally went by. "Audie? Oh, yeah."

"That bad, eh? Ach, don't worry about it. All of us had a first day here at one time. We're all sympathetic. Well, maybe not all... Oh, and my name is JJ." She looked at the sparse contents of Leah's coffee cup and the two mini cups of sugary cream. "Already have a bit too much coffee, maybe?"

"Yup, that and I'm still on Arizona time." She looked at her watch. "According to my internal clock, it's only three-thirty. It's a good thing I spent the last week weaning myself off Mountain Time or I'd be walking into walls instead of tripping over thresholds."

JJ chuckled, then looked up. "Oh, and here's the caustic coffee cooker, KK."

The dark-skinned and slender middle-aged man in surgery scrubs nodded to the women and flipped up the lid on the donut box. "The word's barista or brewer, JJ, not cooker," he said.

"Yeah, yeah," she replied, "but it wouldn't be alliterative that way. KK, say hi to Audie something or other."

"Well, Audie Something-or-other, I guess we won't have to learn your last name. There aren't any other Audies in this hospital. I'm glad you're not an Ashley. It doesn't make a difference that the six who work here spell their names four different ways, they all sound the same. It's still confusing."

"Seven Ashleys," JJ corrected. "They hired a new one – this one male – in the ultrasound lab. We don't have to worry about him since they're already calling him Guy Ashley."

"Maybe I should just go by Madigan. Not many of those around, right?"

KK broke one of the bagels in half and set it on a napkin. "No problem, but Audie works. So, you might as well spill. We'll find out sooner or later. Married or single, looking or hateful, straight or gay?" he asked, then dunked one end of his blueberry bagel into his black coffee.

"Wha? I mean…"

"Ignore him. He's miserable since his boyfriend went on a world cruise with some guy who won the lottery. He's single, hateful, and gay. I'm straight, married, and not looking."

"I hope you aren't looking if you're married," Leah said.

JJ and KK burst out laughing. "Darlin'," KK said, licking a crumb off his index finger provocatively, "way too many married folks are looking."

He saw her slack jaw and explained. "When you get to be my age, you'll see why. Married and unfaithful means the new love interest has no commitment issues – their partners have mortgages, kids in school, and aren't available. And I do mean partners plural. Some of the men and women around here are like players at a casino. They take a few spins on one, then change slot machine and bets. They're not looking for a happy ever after – just to get laid."

"Ew," Leah said, then realized everyone was staring at her, waiting for her report.

She had already anticipated answering the questions asked of any new nurse on a floor. She sucked in a breath of courage, ready to give her fictional account, but all that came out was, "Ju…Justin."

"Sounds like a stall to me," JJ said, opening the box to look for another bakery bit.

"Or a good pair of cowboy boots," KK added, one brow raised in disbelief.

Leah squirmed in her seat. "You two are a tough crowd." *Should I continue? Lying's a lousy way to start a relationship – whether work, casual, or long term. I wouldn't like it if the tables were turned.*

"Justin isn't his name," she said. "Actually, I never knew his real name. How could I? We've never met."

KK chuckled and JJ took out the half blueberry bagel and shut the lid, both looking up to hear the rest of the story.

"My ideal man's name is Justin Case for now. Sometimes he's blond, but that's only when one of those surfer songs from the sixties comes on the radio. The rest of the time, he has dark, mostly straight hair and is a little swarthy. Maybe Hispanic or Native – not pale or even freckled. As for being hateful or looking, I guess I'm ambivalent…or rather, don't care and not looking."

Both of her new co-workers stared at her before turning away, showing with their body language that they didn't believe her.

Leah reached out and put a hand on each of them. "Hey, it's the truth. I just went through hell, watching my dad die from cancer

36

while I was trying to finish clinicals. Then I worked extra shifts like a mad woman to keep busy and, hopefully, sane."

She stopped and laughed. "A mad woman trying to keep sane? Yeah, that was me. All I did was work, grab a salad or fast food, and go to bed early with…"

"With…with?" JJ prompted, leaning forward.

"With a good book," Leah finished.

"Test time," KK said. "What's the name of the book?"

"Which one? I've been rereading all the books in the *Lost* series."

"Oh, you are my new best friend," KK said. "I practically have those books memorized."

"*You* do?" JJ asked. "I'll match you in a quoting contest any day. Either of you."

Leah noticed the room thinning out and looked at her watch. "Time to go to work. Any route better than another to get to the fourth floor at this time of day?"

"Yup," JJ said. "Follow us. Looks like we're going to get to know each other and our good and bad habits sooner than later."

Chapter 5: The Devil's in the Details

Fairbanks Police Station

They clutched each other close, their musky scents intermingling, the heady aroma reminding her of the joining that had just transpired. Her ear pressed against his bare chest through the rip in his new linen shirt and his springy chest hairs tickled her nose. She could both hear and feel the steady thump-thump of his heart, his pectoral muscle rigid with anticipation, a solid assurance that all would be well. At least for a few more minutes.

"Are ye sure this is the man?" he asked. "I ken you read it in yer history book, but do ye think that maybe someone was exaggerating?"

"Hush," she whispered. "They'll hear you."

"Hey, have you ever heard of a company called Little Woman Enterprises?" Arlie asked. "The phone number on the van was duct-taped over."

Bonnie quickly closed the paperback book in her lap and looked up, embarrassed to be caught reading any book on the job, much less the latest and lustiest in the *Lost* series. Arlie's nose was in his smartphone, though, checking out something else and hadn't noticed.

"No, I don't think so," Bonnie drawled, recovering her wit, "but let me look." As the clerk, she was a stickler for details. She checked all the databases she had access to, then paused and tensed, her shoulders rising as she inhaled with the sudden memory.

"Make that a negative on that no," she said. "I mean, there's nothing here, but that name rings a bell. You see, I had a neighbor who started a curbside recycling business a few years back. She had a minivan and pulled a little homemade trailer behind it, picking up cans and papers. She wound up selling out and moving to the Lower Forty-eight. The new company changed the name and expanded to a full-sized fleet. Maybe what you saw was the van she sold before she left."

"Sounds reasonable."

"Yeah, reasonable," she said, "but I doubt it was registered as a commercial vehicle. She was only in business a few months before she gave up and sold out. I don't think there's any way to trace the new owners of the van. I don't even know where she moved. Is this something important? Crap. What was her last name? I mean, do you want me to see if I can track her down and hope she has an old registration, insurance ID card, or something so we can get the VIN?"

"Nah, it's nothing serious. I didn't even check to see if the plates were expired. Some jerk was trying to intimidate a lady at an apartment complex I was checking out. Don't worry about it, but if you do stumble on her contact info somewhere, pass it back to me."

"Got it. I'll add it to my perpetual to-do list."

Arlie went to his desk and turned on his computer. While waiting for it to boot up, he took out his phone and scrolled through his notifications. Nope. Still no pop-up alerts that Charlene was on the move. Either the photo he had fed into the Interpol database wasn't clear enough or she wasn't going near any state, federal, or mass transportation security cameras.

When are you going to stop being such a wuss and go meet her in person? You don't have to tell her you were the sperm donor. Scratch that. You definitely shouldn't let her know! At least use a week of vacation and go to Arizona to see if you can catch a glimpse of the baby she had.

Baby? Chip is nearly three years old now. He can walk and talk, and he's probably even potty trained. Step forward. You've been hiding in the background too long.

39

Hiding is right. As soon as you knew she didn't have a romantic attachment, you should have found a way into her life. Who knows? You might have even become friends.

Yeah, but how would she take it if she found out later you were the kid's bio-dad? Yeah, right. Let it go. Anonymous is all you can ever be to her or the boy.

"Hey, Arlie," a familiar voice called out.

Arlie looked up. "Well, I'll be. What are you doing up here in the Real Great White North, Marc? Anchorage getting too crowded for you?"

"Fugitive Task Force calling. I was looking for one of my ten most wanted when I caught a whiff of a couple of stinkers who have been known to associate with him. Someone saw them in this neighborhood."

Deputy US Marshal Marc Audie pulled out a folder from his briefcase and thumbed through a few papers. He handed a paper copy of two black and white mug shots to Arlie. "Recognize either one of these?"

"Well, I'll be. How did you know I was looking for them? Well, not them, but this one." Arlie tapped on the grainy image of the man who earlier had harassed the web-designer woman at the apartment complex.

"That's Vinnie the Dumb." Marc pointed to the other photo, a man slack jawed as if he was either going to sneeze or was trying to figure out the answer to a difficult question. "And this one's known as Hugo the Dumber."

"Dumb and Dumber?" Arlie asked, then shook his head in amazement. "What are they wanted for?"

"Assault, robbery, grand theft auto, possibly manslaughter, plus assorted back-alley misdemeanors. You know, the kind of crimes that tend to be teething rings for small-town crooks trying to make it into the big time. Those two have the intelligence of a melted snowman, but they got more than their share of grade double-A good luck."

"I saw the one today here." Arlie stepped over to the huge North Star Borough map on the wall and pointed. "Vinnie took off in a mid-nineties candy-apple red Chevy van with the name Little Woman Enterprises painted on it. Turns out Bonnie up front knew the previous owner of the rig. That's not going to help us, though. Little Woman moved back to the Lower Forty-eight a while back."

"From what I know from these two's rap sheets, the vehicle was probably stolen. The only reason the D and D boys would be up here is for a contract. They've had a long string of near misses and are probably looking to score big in a small market," Marc said.

"Or it could be that's all they do: intimidation. I caught Vinnie trying to bully someone this morning. The little old lady stood up to him and he didn't like it. Looked like he was just about to get rough with her when I stepped in. Good thing I was there checking on an apartment. I'm not sure how far he would have pushed it if I hadn't been."

"An apartment? You still renting?" Marc teased, punching Arlie playfully in the shoulder. "Well, here's hoping those two are lazy and haven't opted to grab a new ride. A bright red van should be easy to spot around here. Got a few minutes? I'd like to show you these over a cup of coffee."

Arlie picked up the pile of papers on his desk, scanned through them, then set them back down. "Bonnie, is there anything I need to be in the office for that you know of?"

"Nope. Might as well take that little genius phone of yours outside and enjoy the nice weather while we have it. I'll call or message you if anything pops up."

Arlie turned to his longtime friend. "Bring your folders. Looks like we'll be having our coffee *al fresco,* Marc."

"Do you have a helmet?"

41

Arlie scowled at Marc. "Are you nuts? A vest, yes. Helmet, no."

Marc shook his head. "Not riot gear. I brought my Beemer."

"Beemer?"

The grin on Marc's face was bright enough to awaken Arlie's sense of humor. "You finally got it? That BMW GS?"

"Close. I kicked it up a letter to the GT version. It's more two-person friendly. Come on. I'm itching to see how it handles with the extra weight in the back end."

"Nah, I don't have a helmet. I'll follow you."

"Nope. Not a valid excuse. I have a spare."

"Bonnie, it looks like I'll be limited availability during my coffee break. Catch you in a few."

Marc took Arlie's insulated coffee mug off the desk and jiggled it to check how much was left. "Close enough. We can top it off at the river from my thermos. I want you to see the rest of these," he said, lifting the folder.

Once outside, Arlie spent a few minutes checking out the features on Marc's new ride, then the two were off to the riverside park.

Just as they approached the park entrance, Arlie tapped Marc's shoulder and pointed to the hotel across the street. A candy-apple red van with a crude rattle-can paint job over the former business name was parked next to a semi-truck without a trailer. Marc saw it, too, and drove up next to it.

Arlie hopped off the back of the bike and touched the flat cherry-red color. Tacky. "Not even an hour old," he said to Marc. "And not very well hidden. I'll check with the clerk and see who this belongs to. You move out of sight and watch the van to make sure they don't slip out."

"Not exactly joint task force," Marc said, "but they are on my list. You can bust them for expired plates or stolen vehicle and whatever else applies. Do you want to call it in?"

"Already on it," Arlie said, his phone to his ear. "Hey, Bonnie. Would you run these plates? It's for that red van that used to belong to your friend. It's B-M-Z-8… Damn! One of them's bolting."

Marc took off on his Beemer to stop the culprit's access to the river while Arlie chased him down on foot.

"Freeze!" he yelled, then added, "Halt, stop where you are!" as he continued running.

The man stopped briefly as Marc cut him off, but only long enough to change direction. He darted behind the back end of the motorcycle and scurried through the thick brush and tangle of broken fence to the river's edge.

Splash!

A moment later, a mop of dark hair popped out of the water, arms flailing and mouth sputtering, "D…d…damn!"

Arlie and Marc watched as the man thrashed in the fast-moving Chena, the water's depth unknown but more than a man could stand up in, even if he were able to resist the powerful flow.

Varoom. Putt, putt, putt. Screech!

The two law enforcement officers spun around and saw the candy-apple red van skirt into traffic, tires squealing and horns honking as other drivers swerved to miss it. Arlie brought up his phone. "That's B-M-Z-8-3-8," he said. "And whether it's stolen or not, have it pulled over. Driver's wanted for erratic driving and a dozen or more outstanding warrants." Marc nudge him and nodded to the river. "Oh, and have the boys downriver from The Lodge be on the lookout for a man in the drink. I'd say armed and dangerous, but after his swim, I doubt he could pull a trigger much less hold a gun."

"If it would even fire," Marc said with a snort.

"Okay. Got it. Thanks, Bonnie."

Arlie ended the call. "Those are old plates. He must have taken them off an abandoned vehicle. Dummy. If he's going to steal them, you'd think he'd be smart enough to grab current ones."

Marc laughed. "You'd think. But like I told you, they're known as Dumb and Dumber."

***

Thirty minutes later

"What took you so long?" Vinnie asked, casually smoking a cigarette as he leaned against a mud-spattered, dinged and dented work truck.

Hugo pulled the ratty packing blanket off his shoulders and threw it to the ground. "Me? What were you doing when I had to jump in the river to get away from two cops?"

"I was making sure we still had a way to leave this God-forsaken, mosquito-bitten state! I had to ditch the van and get another ride. Shit! I didn't even take time to grab my shoes. Looks like I'll have to find another pair of size thirteens."

"Make that two pair," Hugo said, pulling off his soggy socks. "That water was so swift, I had to kick off my boots or be pulled under. Pulled under again. Damn! It was ice cold, too. My balls pulled all the way up to my throat." He reached between his legs and patted himself gingerly, probing. "Ah, they're back again."

"Idiot. Of course, the water's cold. It's a melted iceberg. Or glacier. Shit, I can't remember what it is, but it's melted frozen ice," Vinnie said, then gasped.

Hugo's hand was tight on his neck. "Wha…what?" Vinnie croaked, arms up in surrender.

"I told you. Don't. Ever. Call. Me. Idiot," Hugo hissed.

"Okay, okay," Vinnie squeaked, then fell to the ground in a heap as Hugo released him.

As if nothing had happened, Hugo picked up his discarded blanket, shook it out, then wrapped it around his shoulders again. He stepped into the truck on the passenger's side and looked back at Vinnie, still on hands and knees, trying to recover. "Well, what's taking you so long?" he laughed.

Vinnie growled like an angry dog but made it upright. He staggered to the driver's side and held onto the door frame, his head and shoulders stuck through the open window. "If you ever try that again, it'll be the last thing you ever do."

Hugo gave a half-hearty laugh and turned away, mumbling softly so he wasn't heard, "Yeah, that's what you said last time."

"What'd you say?" Vinnie screamed, his last word squeaking out of his bruised voice box.

"I said, we never did get those shrimps." Hugo turned to face him, then added. "I guess we'd better get some shoes first, though, huh?" He looked at his bare feet. "And socks."

Vinnie snorted in disgust, trying to clear his throat at the same time. "Remind me never to come to Alaska again."

A minute later, riding down the highway, Hugo said, "Hey, Vinnie."

"Yeah?"

"I'm reminding you, never come to Alaska again."

Vinnie stomped on the brakes, sending the unbelted, toenail-picking Hugo forward into the dash. "Oops," he said softly.

Just as Hugo sat up and was deciding on whether to punch Vinnie in the ear or shoulder, he spotted the sporting goods store. "Turn right. I mean left. I mean, go that way!" he said and pointed.

Vinnie saw the store at the same time and quickly detoured through a bank's parking lot. "You go to customer service and ask to talk to the shoe department clerk while I go grab a pair."

Hugo frowned. "A pair or a pair of pairs? I thought you needed shoes, too."

"I do, dum… I do, dear baby brother. You know what I like. This time, make sure there aren't any other customers around. You can do your fart thing. That always scares them away."

Hugo started laughing. "I just hope I don't shit my pants this time. Maybe I'll grab some slacks on the way back, too."

"I'll pick up some socks and pay for them, so I don't look suspicious. Just be fast," Vinnie said. He took the keys out of the ignition and locked the door. "Don't want nobody stealing my stolen truck," he whispered to Hugo, then roared with laughter.

"Yeah, don't steal my stolen truck," Hugo repeated loudly.

Vinnie elbowed him.

"Why'd you do that?"

"That's a joke for just you and me, Hugo. Remember, we could get busted and be in real trouble. Play it cool."

"Okay. I promise. Cucumber cool."

***

Twenty minutes and cross trainers, sunglasses, and a pair of sweatpants stolen later, Vinnie and Hugo were on the road.

"Hey, look! There's an all-you-can-eat seafood buffet," Hugo said, reaching across Vinnie's chest to point out the local diner.

Vinnie pushed the meaty arm out of the way with a growl. "Oh, all right. You and that damned stomach of yours. Go in and get us a table. You won't fit in a booth. And make sure it's in the back. We don't want anyone staring at us or being on no security cameras. I gotta call that limey bitch Clotilde and find out whether this Dan or Danny is a guy or a broad."

"Yeah, and either way, she'd better pay us the whole fee," Hugo said, tearing off the XXXL sticker on his new sweats. "She owes us. That was a sneaky trick, just having us pick up the boarding passes to Alaska at the ticket counter, saying the rest was waiting for us."

"Yeah," Vinnie said softly, "I'll never make that mistake again. Nobody gets a job for free. And a trip to Alaska ain't my idea of a vacation, especially since we have to pay for everything."

"Or someone does," Hugo chuckled. He stuck his rolled-up sweatpants under his arm and opened the truck door. "I'll use the

46

john inside to change. It says all you can eat. They never met me, huh? Take your time. I'll be a while."

Vinnie looked down at his phone. The battery was almost dead. Still enough time for a quick phone call, though. He tapped last call and hit redial.

"Hello," a woman answered, her voice bright and British accent thick.

"Yeah, Clotilde lady, this is Vinnie. You sent me to Alaska to off someone named Dan or Danny, right?"

"You imbecile!" she hissed, her tone suddenly caustic. "No names! And no," she added, her attitude suddenly shifting to calm and soothing, "I'd never suggest anyone be 'offed.' You must have the wrong number, sir. I don't know anyone by the name of Vinnie."

"Huh? Oh, yeah. Maybe you know me as Vincent. We never exchanged last names. Anyhow, I'm sure you remember my idiot brother, Hugo. He took notes last time you called. His writing is hard to read. I figured out webstates was supposed to mean websites, and he spelled some stuff wrong, but is this *person of interest*," Vinnie said snidely, "a guy or a dame? I found the web place address here in Fairbanks, just like you said. But it was an old broad livin' there, not a guy. She said it was her business, and the name was Danny, not Dan. I told her that was a guy's name, but she didn't pay me no 'tention. I was just getting ready to give her an attitude adjustment when some redheaded dude pops in."

"Redhair?" Clotilde asked. "Was he Scots?"

"Scotch?" he asked, confused.

"Did…he…have an…unusual…accent?" Clotilde asked, biting back her frustration, speaking slowly so he could understand her the second time around.

"Nope. He sounded like most people around here. He wasn't from Brooklyn, though, and he sure didn't sound like no Limey." He added, "Beggin' your pardon," trying to mimic her speech.

"I'll tell you what I want you to do…"

"Hello, hello?" Vinnie called into the phone. He took it away from his ear. Black screen. The phone was dead.

He stuck the cheap cell phone in his shirt pocket then reached into the glove box, tossing receipts, odd hardware, pens, and a broken pair of reading glasses onto the floorboard. A flattened box of condoms was jammed into the very back. "Hmm, might need these," he said, putting the three-pack in his front pocket and dropping the empty carton onto the trash pile he'd just created.

"All this shit and not one phone charger? What kind of driver is this guy?" He patted the condoms in his pocket. "Well, at least he was prepared for real emergencies." He looked up and saw a brightly painted bus of tourists unloading into the parking lot. The silver-haired riders were milling about, stretching and gathering into little cliques as they lined up to go into the buffet.

"Better get a bite or three before Hugo and the old folks eat it all. Maybe someone will be charging their phone in there. Might get more than just a charger this time. I'm due for an upgrade."

***

"Hang up on me, will you," Clotilde hissed. "You'll never get another nickel out of me." She paused, her mouth swishing back and forth as a smirk arose. "Come to think of it, you never even got a first nickel from me. Those plane tickets were charged to my dear fiancé's airline account. I doubt James ever looks at his bills. Isn't that what the hired help's supposed to do?"

Another glance at her phone and she saw the appointment reminder pop up. "Time to go make myself even more beautiful. I'll tackle this mess in the morning. I want to be clear-headed for teasing the fiancé and impressing the gentry."

***

"Let me see those again, Marc. I think I have an idea where Dumb and Dumber might be." Arlie scanned the photocopies with Vinnie and Hugo's faces, rap sheet, and profile. He handed the sheath back to Marc. "Are you hungry?"

"Not particularly. Why? What did you see that I missed?"

"Hugo is a glutton. He just fell into the Chena River and swam downstream for God only knows how long. What's the first thing someone like that's going to want?"

"Food," Marc said wryly. "And maybe some dry clothes. I know the latter would be first on my list."

"So…" Arlie pulled out his phone and brought up a map of the area where Hugo had slam-dunked his exit. "A few hundred feet downriver there's a bridge, which means pilings and such so he can pull himself out of the water."

"They looked. He wasn't there."

"Or he could have floated further down. He's so big, it might be he wasn't able to make it up the steep bank there. If he didn't succumb to hypothermia, a few hundred yards more and he'd be in shallow water and could just walk out."

Marc reached across and tapped the map. "With that much fat? Shoot, that beluga is well-insulated. And look, there's a sporting goods store right there where he could buy gargantuan-size sweats…"

Arlie slid his finger up a little further. "And there are at least two all-you-can-eat buffets just up the road. I'm betting this guy's after seafood, not pancakes."

"Because they're not paying. Someone else is," Marc agreed. "I'll send a unit to the sporting goods store with pictures. We can go to the Just for the Halibut and wait for them." He paused. "Unless they're already there."

They both made their calls, then Arlie looked at the motorcycle. "Next time, remind me to bring my own ride. I'll let Dottie sit in the sissy saddle."

49

Marc laughed. "Dottie ride behind me? Are you kidding? We both got one of these. As soon as I catch that runaway I hope Vinnie and Hugo lead me to, we're taking the girls to her Mom's and riding down to Homer."

"Must be nice having a wife who shares the same interests as you," Arlie said, then realized he sounded whiny. He grabbed the spare helmet and climbed on behind Marc. "I mean, you sure got lucky with her."

"Luck had nothing to do with it. She told me I never had a chance. Funny. I thought the same thing about her," he joked, then jumped on and throttled up to punctuate the comment.

The two rode past the sporting goods store, saw a trooper was already there, and proceeded to the second biggest draw in the North Star Borough: the all-you-can-eat seafood buffet.

"I'll go in first this time," Marc said. "They know your face, or at least Vinnie does."

"I'll call it in and head around back. Don't spook 'em too bad. I'd hate to try and restrain that big one by myself."

"At least he probably won't be armed. River water and Rugers don't get along very well. I doubt Vinnie would let him use his, or one of his. Scuttlebutt is, there's still sibling rivalry raging between those two."

Bypassing the masses of seniors queuing up in three lines, Marc strode into the café, helmet in hand. He glanced around the dining area, then at the hostess. Rather than show her his badge and explain his mission, he flashed her a smile, adding a wink just in case she was a tough one. "Come, come, right in," she said. "You don't want to wait for them," nodding to the two old ladies at the head of a long queue, their mouths open to argue that the biker had cut in line.

"Thanks," Marc said to the hostess, then looked back at the scowling biddies. "I won't be too long. I promise not to eat all the crab." Another smile and a wink, and the two old women were giggling like schoolgirls.

"I think he's one of those reality TV stars," one said.

"Nah, I think that's Tom Petty…and he winked at me!"

Eyes squinted to adjust to the dimness, Marc spotted a big guy in the back, blocking the emergency exit door. Hugo or an innocent?

The man's face was a scant two inches over his plate, shoveling fistfuls of fries into his gaping maw. Cheeks puffed to full, he sat back and used gravity to assist in swallowing the food. He guzzled half his soda in one long slurp, smacked his lips, and picked up a massive king crab leg.

Eyes now adjusted to the light, Marc was certain this was Hugo. Was Arlie in place? And where was Vinnie? Should he wait before making his move? Yes. Patience, man. Haste translates to, 'Hasta luego,' in Fugitive Speak.

A vicious smile spread across Hugo's face. Using both hands, he snapped the foot-long crab leg in half, pulling it apart with an unnatural glee.

Marc cringed at the image it brought to mind, remembering the stories he'd heard about Hugo and his 'attitude adjustments.' A gentle hand touched his arm and he quickly stepped back.

"Would you like a booth or a table," the middle-aged Asian lady asked, her dark eyes sparkling in an answer to his earlier wink.

"Oh, I'm waiting for someone," Marc said and stepped back into the shadow of the corner. "I'll just wait here if you don't mind," he said and didn't wait for her answer.

A few minutes of watching Hugo demolish four plates of food had Marc's stomach roiling. The man was a human garbage disposal, even though the fare was first class. It could have been spoiled cabbages and moldy field corn and he would have consumed it just as savagely. Marc took out his phone. 'Where R U?' he texted Arlie.

'Out back. There's a traffic jam. Wait. He'll show.'

Hugo finally pushed away from the table, licking the remains of lemon meringue pie from his thumb and fingers, drying them on his sweatpants. He stood up, looked around the room, and shrugged, a silent chuckle and head nod confirming he was sated. "You snooze, you lose, big brother." He reached in his pocket, found a few coins, slapped them on the table, then took back the quarter.

Out of Hugo's line of sight, Vinnie walked in the front door and blinked, eyes adjusting to the light. To be sure he wasn't seen, Marc slipped behind the tall plastic dieffenbachia to wait and listen.

Hugo approached the cashier just as the hostess greeted Vinnie. "I left you some," he called over and added a rude chuckle. "But I can't say the same for those old fogeys. I had to wrestle the last piece of pie from one old lady." He paused and amended his last remark. "Well, not wrestle, but I did have to snarl."

Vinnie rolled his eyes then looked to the hostess. "I guess it's just dinner for one, then. Oh, and that table in back will be fine."

"You have to prepay, sir," she said, hand out. "That will be twenty-nine ninety-five."

Vinnie started to protest, then realized it wasn't his money, and handed her a credit card.

She ran it through the card reader, then her eyes widened and face paled. She looked up. "It says declined." She bit her bottom lip, not wanting to add that the card reader also said to seize the card and call authorities.

Vinnie saw the look. Time for Mr. Nice Guy. "Oh, I'm sorry. That's my old one. I canceled it before I moved up here. You know how it is. Data breaches and scams are rampant." He pulled out the rubber-banded bundle of credit cards from his pocket, then realized she was staring at it. "Try this one."

She took the card and read the name. Akito Tanaka. She looked up again with a sick smile. This card had been stolen from her father two days earlier. She ran the possible scenarios through her head, balancing the loss of the cost of one meal against a confrontation with a thief who just might be dangerous.

She handed the card back to him. "No need to pay for today's meal. You're customer number two thousand. All you can eat for free," she said, a cold sweat running down her hairline into her ear. She swiped it away. "Any table you want."

Vinnie left, Hugo following behind him.

As soon as the brothers were gone, Marc stepped out. "Are you okay?" he asked the hostess.

"No. I mean, he's a thief. I didn't want to ask him for a third card and raise a stink." She plopped down on the stool behind her. "I think I'm going to faint. Maybe I'd better call a cop first."

"You just did, darlin'," Marc said. He took out his phone and texted Arlie. 'Ready? Stolen cards, too.'

'Back up's here. I'll be right in.'

Marc looked up. Arlie's hair was shining autumn red and gold, backlit by the daylight streaming through the open door. "Hey, Hana," he said to the hostess. "Someone giving you grief?"

In less than a second, Hana had her arms wrapped around Arlie. "Oh, yes, yes…"

"Well, then let me do my job," Arlie said, gently patting her back with reassurance. "Maybe I'll pop in after my shift for a late dinner. Save me a piece of cherry pie."

***

Hugo followed Vinnie to the back of the room, pausing to grab a fresh cup for another soda refill. "Not bad," Hugo said. "You got lucky. I thought she had you for sure."

Vinnie put his hand to his forehead then looked at the neat stacks of warmed plates, the buffet trays half-filled with real food, their smell heady. "I'm either getting sick or living on fries and soda is catching up to me. Yeah, lucky or maybe she recognized me."

"Huh?" Hugo asked and giggled nervously. "Oh, yeah. She didn't look the type, but she could have been a wrestling fan. Yup, that was probably it."

Vinnie piled the food high on his plate, tingles rising on his arms and up the back of his legs at the thought of how great scalloped potatoes and shrimp scampi would taste.

Just as he sat down, he felt a strong hand on his arm. "Not so quick there, buddy," Arlie said.

"I'm not Buddy," he protested and grabbed his fork with the other hand. "Leave me the hell alone. I'm eating."

Arlie came around and sat across from him, his face in Vinnie's. "Remember me?"

The fork loaded with shrimp and peppers just inches from his mouth, Vinnie looked up. "Who?" He blinked several times as he focused on the man in front of him, trying to place him. "You! Ah, shit. I didn't do nuthin' wrong."

"Maybe you didn't this morning, but just now you tried to pass off two stolen credit cards. We have to bring you and your brother in."

"He ain't my brother," Vinnie protested, glancing up and glaring at Hugo, now subdued with hands behind his back, a fair-haired man in tactical gear standing behind him.

"Yeah, he's not my brother," Hugo agreed. "Because we got different moms. And how do you know who we are, anyhow?"

Three more troopers came in, suited up with vests, weapons, and all the accouterments of their trade, an impressive presentation of force and unity.

"To protect and to serve," an old man's voice called out from one of the booths. "Go get 'em, guys and gal!"

54

Slight smiles spread across the enforcers' faces and Vinnie and Hugo's shoulders sagged. "Can I at least finish my lunch?" Vinnie asked, reaching for the fork Arlie had forced from his hand.

"Nope. At least, not with utensils," Arlie said, grabbing his hand and cuffing him behind his back. "Don't worry. They'll feed you down at the station. Eventually."

Vinnie leaned forward and scarfed up his food like a ravenous dog at a plate of wet scraps, turning his head to get one last slurp of noodles before being jerked up to his feet by the mega-trooper behind him.

Hugo laughed and said, "Yeah, kind of hard to break open king crab legs with your hands behind your back, huh? Don't worry. I ate enough for both of us."

Vinnie lunged at his brother but was caught up short by the two of the officers.

"Sorry about the mess, Hana," Arlie said on the way out the door, the last person in the line of assorted felons and law enforcement.

"The food is no problem," she replied. "Thank *you,* for taking care of the biggest mess – them!"

***

Brrg! Brrg!

Dani rushed to the phone, tripping on the throw rug and breaking a nail on the counter as she reached out to save herself from performing a spread-eagle bellyflop on the kitchen floor.

"Hello!" she snarled. "Oh, hi, officer… Oh, it's *Detective* Biggar? Okay, just Arlie. I'm sorry. It's me, not you. Oh, you caught him? Oh, and then he got away? Lucky for him, but not so much for the troopers. Wait, there's two of them? Yikes! Okay. I'll make sure I keep the doors locked. No, I have no idea why he was here. My address isn't published anywhere, at least in association with my web designing business. I mean, he said that's why he was

55

here, but if he's a crook, no telling. Thanks for the warning. I hope you catch him. Or catch him again."

Dani set the phone down gently. The screen was cracked but still intact. "Why would anyone want to bother me? I'm not rich or young and foxy. Not for the last forty years, at least on the young part. Never been rich and beauty is in the eyes of the beholder. At least back then, I wasn't wrinkly. Or so big."

Chapter 6: The Contract

Same time, London

"Idiot!" Clotilde huffed. "Hang up on me, will you!" She squinted at the screen, looking for the name on the caller ID, then remembered that would give her wrinkles. "I don't need reading glasses to verify that was one of those Yank lamebrains Maurice recommended. Are all Americans that thick or just those two?"

She looked around the room. Yes, still alone. She stamped her feet in an adult version of a temper tantrum and gritted her teeth, stifling a shout just in case the walls in this old place were thin and someone was around.

"That's it. I'm going back to Maurice for a refund." She yanked open the bedroom door, then realized that's not how a real lady would act. Taking a deep breath, she tried to channel Lady Di. "I'll be demure and refined. Genteel and so sweet, the heathen's teeth will hurt."

Clotilde walked down the hall with a practiced sashay to the kitchen where the help spent their time socializing when not otherwise engaged. "Charles, take me to The Rocks," she blurted at the chauffeur as her cool evaporated like seawater on lava. "Now."

The Rocks? The driver held back his shock at the neighborhood she'd chosen but did as he had been instructed: drive Miss Clotilde anywhere she wanted. It wasn't his job to be the babysitter to the irascible wife-apparent of the Melbourne estate's second in line. James was smart. He'd figure it out eventually. Maybe. Hopefully, before he wed her. Or at least, before she found a way to siphon off the family fortune.

After the fifteen-minute drive to one of the most crime-infested parts of London, he sighed and said dryly, "We're here, madame."

Clotilde started to correct his designation, to tell him she was a mademoiselle, not a madame, but decided to let it slide. As soon as she was lady of the house, she'd fire the old buzzard. "Wait here for me. I'll just be a moment."

The chauffeur opened the door for her and held back his smirk, his bushy mustache twitching.

Plop!

"You bastard," she screeched. "You parked next to that puddle on purpose!"

"Oh, my," he said, feigning shock. "Here, I think I have a rag somewhere. I'll clean it up…"

"Get back, oaf. I'll deal with you later."

"Yes, madame," he said, nodding to hide the glee he felt from addressing her as a matron.

Clotilde called out, "Maurice! Maurice!" as she walked up the street as if searching for a lost cat.

In a flash, a rail-thin youth popped up beside her. "Whatcha want, lady?"

"That's Lady Clotilde," she huffed, looking behind the boy to see if he was alone.

"Maurice ain't here. And if you want somethin' from him, you'd better ask me. I'll be takin' over the territory when he retires," he said, bony tee-shirt covered chest puffed out in pride.

"You?" she squeaked. "But you're just a boy."

"Hey, either you want somethin' or you don't. Which is it?"

Clotilde pursed her lips and gritted her teeth, holding in a scream. She couldn't demand her money back for the job Vinnie and Hugo didn't finish because she'd never given Maurice so much as a pence. Best to bring out her wiles and see if this young one was susceptible to a woman's flirt, whether he was truly the heir of the underworld dynasty or not.

"I'm looking," she said slowly and seductively, batting her eyes and smiling, "to contract an agent for a *business arrangement* in Greensboro. Can you help me?"

"Never heard of the place," he shot back with a sneer. He paused and asked, "Is it in Scotland?"

"No, no, dear sweet…" Clotilde bit off the word child. Surely that would be an insult to him. "Greensboro is in North Carolina. That's in America."

"The Colonies?" he asked.

"Yes, they were called the Colonies…about two-hundred and fifty years ago."

Bzz. Bzz.

The youth pulled a cell phone from the hip pocket of his torn and tattered low-slung jeans, checked the text, and grinned. "Ah, yes. Greensboro, USA. I did hear tell of a man and his sons who'd do just about anything – or anyone – you wanted. Theft, grift, a little runnin' of the ladies maybe…"

"Who are they and how much?"

Bzz. Bzz.

The teen looked at his phone again, then up at her. "Ah, today's your lucky day. Since this is the first day of me bein' in charge, this won't cost you a farthing. The old man you want to talk to is named Atholl MacLeod the Seventh, but everyone knows him as Sept." He wiped his nose on the palm of his hand and reached out. "Give me your phone and I'll type in his number."

He saw her tsk of disgust and rubbed his hand on the leg of his pants. He stuck out his hand again, grinned mischievously, then winked.

She jerked in surprise at the apparent flirt then smiled demurely. *Be nice until you have the numbers, Clotilde. Don't slam the door until the name and number are in your possession.*

"Thank you, dear," she said and patted his cheek like a puppy. "I'll remember you in my prayers."

The lad watched as she walked away, her pace quickening and arms now flailing as she tried to hail the limousine driving right at her. Unseeing, the chauffeur's eyes were staring straight ahead and by the twisted grin, intentionally ignoring her.

Maurice watched from behind the boy, then spoke, his stealth shocking his nephew. "Looks like she has friends all over the place."

"Geez, Unc! Hey, what's with the name and number you had me give her? Is it made up?"

"Nope. Sept and his two sons make Dumb and Dumber look like Albert Einstein and Stephen Hawking." He saw the blank look on the boy's face. "They make Vinnie and Hugo look like geniuses."

The boy nodded and laughed. "Yeah, well, do you think she'll come back?"

"Nope. I'm sure this is costing her more in lost time and frustration than if she'd paid a real professional. Some people don't realize that when you get something for free, you get what you pay for."

***

"Take me home, Charles," Clotilde said as she settled in the back seat, the ice in her voice as chilly as her wet and muddy feet.

"Yes, madame," he said, nose twitching. He turned on the blinker and headed for the bypass to her house.

"Not my old one," she snarled. "My new home."

"Oh, you want to go to the Melbourne Estate, then…"

She looked up and caught his reflection in the rearview mirror and growled softly.

"Of course, madame."

Once back into her room at the seventeenth-century manor, she kicked off her flats, turned on the tub, and grabbed the laptop she'd told James she just *had* to have. "Let's see what I can find out about some of these people…"

She picked up her scribbled note with names and dates from the ancient letter. "Damn! I should have taken a photo of it. That way, I'd have a copy." She tossed in two bath bombs, then decided to make it three. It had been a rough day and she deserved to be pampered. Too bad this family was more modern and hadn't offered her a personal maid and dresser. Those would come after she wed James. The poor sucker.

"Nothing. Not a damn thing on Atholl MacLeod the Seventh. No social media, police records… Oh, wait! I'll check the genealogy sites. Seven generations with the same name. Maybe one of them is famous."

A minute later, she found him. Or at least a few of his ancestors. She scanned through the list, then started reading articles and biographies of Atholl Grant MacLeod the Fourth, the Civil War butcher. She looked up when she heard the dribble, plop, plop of water spilling onto the flagstone floor.

"Damn! The tub's too full now." After setting the laptop on the dressing table, she reached into the water and pulled out the wadded washcloth she used to block the overflow. What good was a bath if a person couldn't fill it to the rim? Or at least, to the rim when she was in it. She let the tub drain for a minute, eager to continue reading about the rogue ancestors of her new champion in America. "Just a little bit more…" she whispered, then stuck the cloth back in.

Satisfied with the depth, she set her silk bonnet over her perfect coif, then slid into the clawfoot porcelain tub, the heady aroma of jasmine and roses tickling her nose. "Maybe three bombs was one too many," she said just as a sneeze exploded.

Knock, knock.

"Are you all right, mum?" the maid called out.

"Yes, thank you," she answered, then said under her breath. "You old snoop."

Scenarios of how she should approach this man Sept raced through her head as she soaked, then slowed as her muscles relaxed in the warmth of Epsom-salted water. "The scrap of paper said map and the letter said James met a man on his trip to America. He's there now. Maybe that's where the map comes from. That map has to be the key to Lord Martin the Mush-brained Melbourne's scam. I'll just tell MacLeod that the map leads to gold and jewels. Yeah. Greed ought to be enough motivation. If I do this right, I can convince him and his sons that they'll get half the treasure as payment, much more than a couple hundred quid for pinching a piece of paper."

Clotilde sighed deeply and lay her head back on the rolled-up towel. "Sometimes I'm so smart, I amaze myself."

***

"Who's this?" Sept growled into the phone.

"Excuse me?" Clotilde asked, too stunned to be angry.

"I said, who-is-this? And if yer hard of hearin', what are ye doin' talking on a phone."

Clotilde silently counted to five – ten would take more patience than she had today – and started her spiel. "If this is Sept MacLeod, I have a business proposition for you."

"Weel, why dinna ye say so," he said, and stepped outside of the minimarket into the parking lot where he'd have more privacy. "Sorry fer bein' short with ye, ma'am. Lots of calls comin' in, wantin' me to buy timeshares or some such nonsense. So, what're ye proposin'?"

"First, are you familiar with the Greensboro, North Carolina area?"

"I could spit there from here. What next?"

She gulped in horror at his crudeness, then realized the slob was a prime bucket of clay for her, just waiting to be molded. And manipulated. She could take advantage of him over the phone, all without having to wink, wiggle, or feign attraction. Well, she still might use the last one, just for fun...

"I said, what next?"

"Sorry. I had to find a stronger signal. Can you hear me now?" she asked, scanning the webpage story of the MacLeod family history and their criminal influence across America and the United Kingdom, both civil and military.

"Yeah, I hear ye."

"I'm looking for a map. It's a treasure map, but it takes a special key to read it. I know where it's supposed to be, but I don't know exactly when it will be there."

"How much?" Sept asked.

"For the job? I was figuring we could split the gold and jewels right down the middle. You for retrieving it, my half for giving you the information…"

Sept interrupted. "Not that. How much is the treasure worth?"

Clotilde took a deep breath, trying to keep her cool with the brute. "It's worth a million, easily. It's an old treasure, though, so it's probably worth a lot more in today's money. As I said, you have to have the key."

"Yeah, yeah. I heard ye the first time." Sept tapped his fingers on the old van he had been using for the past six months. Eight and Niner – his sons – could help with this job. Too bad Benji and Wee Michael had taken off. They could have helped, too. Nah. They'd just be in the way. Stealing never sat right with Benji. Good riddance to the big redheaded kid, and his scrawny little girly-boy best friend.

Clotilde cleared her throat loudly to get his attention. "Excuse me. Are you interested? If not, I have a few other numbers I can call," she lied. "You wouldn't want to pass up a good deal like this."

"Why don't you do it?" Sept asked, suspicious of her pushy nature.

"I'm a lady," Clotilde said in her thickest and most aristocratic accent. "I don't push people around to get goods."

"Yeah, yeah. There are easier ways, right? Hey, what's yer name, anyhow?"

"Just call me Lady C. I'll text you the address, so you don't get it wrong. As I said, I don't know which year, but I do know the date. It's on Halloween."

"Wait. What? That's," Sept put down the phone and started counting on his fingers. "August, September, October." He picked it up again. "That's three months from now!"

"Or it could be a year and three months, or two years and three months, or... You get the idea, right? Just consider this easy money. The man who has the map is a small fellow. I believe he works with the reenactors at one of the War of Independence historical sites. You know, what you Americans call the Revolutionary War?"

"I ain't no American," Sept growled. "I'm Scots but my family's been stuck over here fer most of the last two hundred years. But whether I was born in Cleveland or Clackmannan, I'm still Scots. And don't ye forget it."

"Yes, sir," Clotilde said, hiding a snicker behind her hand. "Now, you have my phone number on your caller ID. Don't lose it. Once you have the map, let me know. I'll send a courier for it so I can...um...use the key on it."

"Okay, but I have one question. What's this map made of that it'd have a keyhole in it? Is it a box or somethin'?"

"No, key as in legend, like a code."

"Oh, like on them decoder rings in cereal boxes. Right? Gotcha. Hey, how about sendin' me a few hundred bucks to tie me and the boys over for three months? Ye can take it out of my share later."

"All right," she said and picked up the Lamy pen on James's desk. "Give me the address. It'll take a few days…"

"Not if ye wire it to a Sprawl-Mart. Just give 'em my name and a keyword, and we're set. Oh, and maybe make the keyword yer name. That'll work. They won't let ye use mine 'cause that's who it's goin' to."

"I can do that. It should be there by morning."

Click.

"What an idiot! Then again, he doesn't need brains to grab a map, just fast hands. At least he knows how to read." Clotilde paused and her stomach dropped. "I sure hope he knows how to read."

***

Two days later

Grumble.

The noise of her stomach complaining woke Clotilde from a deep sleep. Fumbling to remove her sleep mask, she rolled over and looked at the clock on her bedstand. Nine a.m. Too early.

"I don't want to wake up. And I sure don't want to be hungry," she said aloud, hoping the verbal suggestion to her body would work.

Roil, grumble, rolling-thunder growl!

She argued back. "Shut up. You'll get food when you lose two more pounds. I *will* look stunning – absolutely perfect – in that gown. Hmph. Even if it isn't on a Lady Di level. Bastards wanted too much for one of those. Still, it was decent of them to make me an inflated estimate for the one they designed for me."

Crabby but resigned, she wiggled into the down-filled duvet one more time, arched her back luxuriously, then swung her feet over and into her mink-lined slippers. Suddenly, she was thinking about her wedding dress again. "That idiot James has no idea how much bridal attire costs. The sap. It was pathetic how easy it was to trick him into paying for it. He's too dim to discover it only cost a tenth of what he gave me. My sweet hunk Randy and I will have so much fun this weekend in Cannes with the difference." She sighed. "James will stay here, absorbed in his books, believing I'm such a wonderful daughter, visiting my dear old mum in the country again. *Pbbt!* Yeah, I'll be screwing my eyes out with Randy. I'm so lucky he's such an understanding boyfriend. It's not every man who'd let his woman spend so much time with a fake but real fiancé."

Clotilde picked up the insulated pot of coffee and poured a small amount into the frilly porcelain teacup. "Gah! How can anyone drink this mud without sweetener?" She tore off a piece of tissue and swallowed it with a sip of water. "There. That ought to quiet you, tummy. No food until I'm rail thin." She squirmed at the thought of her lover. "Randy does like bangin' them bones."

Knock, knock.

"Are you awake, ma'am?" the maid asked.

"Yes, I'm awake now," Clotilde said testily, then quickly put on her lady of the year attitude. "Yes, my dear. I'm up and getting ready to face the day. Is there something you need?"

"Oh, no, ma'am. We're fine. I mean, I'm fine. It's just that we have a funeral to go to, my brother and I. I can make you a fine breakfast before we leave. Oh, and I wasn't sure if you were needing to go anywhere today. Charles was coming with us, too."

"No, no," Clotilde said through the door, rolling her eyes. "I'll be fine here, all by myself. Oh, and I don't have an appetite right now. I'm sure I can find a biscuit if I get peckish."

"Thank you, ma'am. Have a pleasant day."

"You, too," Clotilde said, then remembered where the serving staff was going. "I mean, my condolences on your loss. Ta ta."

She put on her robe, then stood by the door and waited for the sound of receding footsteps to disappear. Stepping into the vast hallway, she looked up and down, then went to the top of the stairs and saw the door shut behind the trio.

"Hooray!" she hissed in a muted shout. "The house is mine, mine, mine! James won't be back until next week at the earliest. A funeral and all the weeping and wailing will last until dark, at least. That gives me..." Clotilde counted on her fingers, then gave up. "More than three hours to see where Marty hides his treasures."

Clotilde spent the next two hours picking up and putting down myriads of knickknacks in the older man's rooms, pressing paneling to find secret passages, looking in closets. Just before giving up, she stubbed her toe on a thick bearskin rug. "Oh, it wouldn't be that simple, would it?"

Down on all fours, she pulled up the corner of the felt backing and inspected the wooden floor. Impressed into one section was a brass ring. She tugged on it and discovered Marty's hiding place: a recessed cubby.

She pawed through the sparse memorabilia – a pair of booties, a christening gown, and a dried-out bouquet of posies – to find what was hidden beneath. "What the hell? A book? And a romance novel, at that!"

Clotilde read the description in large font on the back of the book. "Lost. A time travel romance... Pbbt!"

She turned the book over again and looked at the redhaired and bare-chested cover model closer. "I'd bang him, whether Randy was my man or not. Then again, with this guy, I'd say yes to a threesome..."

First putting the mementos back, she took the book and snuggled into the big leather chair at Marty's desk, ready to read. She realized she was squinting again, even with the lamp shining right on the print. Rummaging through the top drawer, she found them: a pair of reading glasses.

"So, what do we have here..."

Chapter 7: Deception

He watched as she threaded her way through the bracken, stepping over fallen limbs and rotted logs toward the creek. She paused at a boulder. A quick twig and leaf removal using the edge of her shawl prepared her dressing table. Or undressing table.

The day was warm. Her shoulder covering was not for warmth but for modesty. What she was doing now certainly didn't belong in that category.

Instead of using it as a table, she sat upon the broad granite mass as if it was a throne. Now seated, she lifted one foot in front of her and leaned forward, pressing her breasts against her corset, the round milky white mounds rising like bread on a warm day. She lazily untied the laces of the moccasins she had made for herself.

The sight of the long expanse of her lily-white skin, bared ankle to knee, would have aroused any man. Her fluid movements were more an erotic dance of the hands than a shoe shucking. He held his breath as she pulled off the first moccasin and stocking at the same time, dropping them to the ground without a care. She shifted sideways and brought up the other leg. Five long, ivory and obscenely titillating toes grasped the boulder beneath her. Oh, that it would be him beneath her! She tucked her delectable foot close to her bottom, her milk-white thigh now exposed. The entrance to her pleasure was barely covered by the fullness of her skirts, the homespun petticoat preventing him from seeing more of his wife.

Was this right? Should he be spying on her?

It truly wasn't espionage, he justified. He was ensuring her safety, appreciating her fine form, and letting her have some of what she called her 'alone time.' Time she said she needed to reflect on her situation. Whatever that was. Would she ever tell him how she came to be in Scotland? A woman so beautiful and spirited should not be left without a husband to protect her. And to pleasure her…

"Not bad," Clotilde said. "But give me a hot, steamy video any day. This soft porn stuff is for pussies." She chuckled at her play on words. "Yeah, give me the hard stuff with André the Real Giant. Now that guy would make any woman squeak."

Clotilde looked through the drawers of his lordship's desk to see if she could find anything interesting. Zip. Nothing. Lord Marty the Numbskull's belongings were as boring as he was.

"Shoot! I forgot to send money to that idiot, Sempt, was it?" She looked at her phone, growled at not being able to see, and picked up Marty's glasses. "Sept," she read, verifying the name, then took a sticky note and wrote it out in big block letters. "I'll send you a few pence to tie you over. Two days late doesn't make much difference – or it shouldn't. Just don't cross me, you mangy Scot."

***

Clotilde rolled James's debit card over and under her fingers like a magician with a quarter. "Too big to hide behind someone's ear, but all I need are these numbers. Two hundred US dollars won't be enough to raise any suspicion, I'm sure. I'll keep adding to my wish list while James is gone. My very own limitless card."

***

"Where is that money!" Sept screamed.

"Careful, Pa," Eight said. "We're runnin' out of Sprawl-Marts. We've been kicked out of pretty near every one we've been to."

"Are you sure she said Greensboro?" Niner asked, then took two steps back just in case his Pa had more temper to lose.

"It doesn't make no difference which one it is. All I need to tell 'em is my name and the code word."

"Are you sure you got the code word right?" Eight asked, then moved behind a tree. He'd been thumped too many times in the last two days, too.

"Yer both idiots! I swear, yer mother must have been messin' around with some foreigner because ye sure don't have my brains."

"But we look just like ya, Pa…" Niner said, wiping under his drippy nose with a grimy hand.

Bzz. Bzz.

Sept pulled the cell phone out of the front pocket of his coveralls and looked at the caller ID. "Don't recognize the number," he said and started to put it back.

"Maybe it's them guys at the Sprawl-Mart. The last one said he'd call us when the money came through," Eight said.

"Yeah, huh," Niner agreed.

Sept flipped open the phone. "It's yer nickel," he said, grinning broadly at the fifty-year-old joke. "It is? How much? Well, why can't ye tell me? Oh, all right. Me and my boys'll be right down. Which store are ye at? Okay then. We'll just get to the nearest one. Oh, and thanks fer the call."

The patriarch put the phone back and smiled, a dark brown splotch of chew stuck across his bottom teeth. "Come on, boys! Let's celebrate. And who knows – heh, heh, heh – we might even do the job after we get the money."

***

Thirty minutes later

"You said it was her name. Are you sure you don't remember it?" the clerk asked.

"Look, it was two days ago when I talked to her. I remembered it when I came in then, but ye wouldn't give it to me. The money, that is."

"Look, sir, let me talk to my manager. I think we might be able to work something out," she said. "I'll be right back."

The frustrated clerk locked up her till and walked to the back of the store and the manager. "Sir, he's back again. It's the same man, I'm sure, who they alerted us to in the storewide email. It's only two-hundred dollars, sir. Shoot, I'll bet everyone who's had to deal with him will kick in a few bucks just to get rid of him and keep him from coming back. He did say it was a British woman's name. Honestly, I don't think he wrote it down because he can't write. He started the form to withdraw the money but was scratching out so many mistakes. I wound up filling in everything for him except the signature."

"What's the keyword?"

"Clotilde, sir."

"Give him the money. I probably couldn't remember that name either, much less figure out how to spell it. Here, I'll go with you. I'd like to see what this guy looks like. He sure has everyone talking."

The store manager led the way back to the wire services kiosk, grinning. There was no doubt in his mind who the problem person was. He was picking his nose, wiping an unseen blob of something on the bib of his grimy coveralls.

"I think we've found the problem, Mr. MacLeod. Now, if you'll just sign here to acknowledge receipt of the funds."

Sept looked up and asked, "Huh?"

"Oh, you're right," the manager said, turning his back so Sept didn't see him fight a full-blown belly laugh. "I have to give you the money first." He opened the till and pulled out ten twenty-dollar bills. "Will this work or would you rather have two one-hundred-dollar bills?"

"Can I have both?" Sept asked and laughed, his sons joining him with thigh-slapping guffaws.

The manager grimaced and shook his head. "Twenties, then?" and offered him the form for his signature while keeping a tight grip on the cash.

71

"Oh, all right," Sept said and bent to sign his name. A long half-minute later, he stood up straight and looked at his handiwork. "Not bad and gettin' better all the time." He turned to his sons. "Come on, boys. Let's go have some fun."

***

"Oh! You're back," Clotilde squeaked in shock. "I thought you were going to be gone another week."

James bent in for a warm welcome home kiss from his fiancée, but only received a quick, distracted little peck on the cheek. "I'm sorry, dear," Clotilde said, turning away from him to hide her shock. "I've had a bit of a cold. I wouldn't want you to get sick."

"I was done with my business and thought you and I might be able to pop over to Cannes for a week before the wedding. You know, maybe a little pre-wedding honeymoon?" he asked.

Clotilde brought her hand in front of her face to push away an imaginary blonde tress, hiding her look of fear and hoping he didn't notice she was already golden tan from spending three days on the beach there.

She gasped as inspiration hit, a precocious pout added to help sell the excuse and put the blame on him. "I wish I'd known you wanted to go earlier. I already spent as much time as I should under the tanning lights. I wanted to be just the right color to show off that beautiful gown you let me have commissioned." She tiptoed up and gave him a preemptive peck on the cheek. "You're the best."

James shrugged, hoping the insecure feeling crawling up his arms was just pre-marriage jitters, the traditional cold feet most grooms got, and not his gut instinct ready to give him a swift knockout punch. Whether it was a sixth sense or just luck, he'd always listened to that still small voice and either came out ahead or averted danger. His decision to marry Clotilde kept a perpetual slight tinkle of 'danger-danger' bells going in his head. If the 'you're doomed' gong ever went off, he'd run in the other direction – fast.

It was almost magical how she kept him perpetually hot and bothered, teased and turned on to the point he thought he'd pop. She always backed down at the last moment – said she was old fashioned, still a virgin – and wanted to wait until she was married to go 'all the way.' As difficult as it was, he'd respect her wishes and wait. One thing for sure, even though his experience with women was limited, he knew he'd never felt this way before.

Clotilde saw James's eyes glazing over. No telling what he was thinking about. She didn't care. She could steer the topic of any conversation her way. "Ahem."

"Yes, dear?"

"Are you sure your grandfather won't be joining us for the wedding? I know it's a small affair, but with your father recently deceased and all, well…"

"What are you really asking, Clotilde?"

"Why don't we just say damn it all and elope? Just go to the judge. I can still wear my gown. I don't care if I turn heads…" Clotilde gave 'the pout' again, covering her glee at her impending coup with feigned desire for him.

James felt his nether regions tingle. "How soon?"

"Well, since we already have the license, we could probably do it tonight…" Clotilde saw James's eyes widen in horror. *Too soon.* "Of course, I'm teasing. The weather is supposed to be nice this weekend. We could invite a few friends over for a small banquet and garden games – maybe lawn darts or croquet – or just the ceremony with drinks and *hors d'oeuvres*." She ran her hand up his sleeved arm lightly, her touch a barely perceptible tickle. "That way, we could get to the 'good part' of being married sooner."

"Ahem."

73

James looked up at the throat clearing. Charles – the family chauffeur, confidant, and all-around go-to person when a household crisis arose – was standing in the hallway, a small silver salver in hand, an ivory-colored calling card resting on it. He'd been so enraptured in his fiancée's diatribe, he hadn't heard him come in.

Clotilde hadn't seen him either, her back to the open door. She spun around, angry that her spellcasting had been interrupted. She felt the rush of cold air as her actress persona split apart for a moment as his flicker of disgust pierced her. She quickly applied the character patch of a woman's go-to remedy: a lady's faint.

"Oh, dear," she said and swooned, hoping James would catch her before she hit the floor.

He reached out and grabbed her, pulling her close. "I got you."

His strong arms supporting her felt uncharacteristically good. Clotilde shuddered at the thought of truly caring for James and buried the fleeting tickle. "Oh, Charles," she gasped. "You gave me such a fright."

"Are you alright, my dear?" James asked with deep concern and a tinge of fear.

Clotilde smiled weakly, burying her sneer of victory to be enjoyed later in private. "I…I think so. Maybe I'd better lie down for a bit."

"I'll be right back, Charles," James said, his arm wrapped around her rib cage, alarmed at how thin she was. "Please, tell whoever is calling I'll be out after I see to a situation."

A flicker of a frown flashed across Clotilde's face at his words. James hadn't seen it, but Charles had. *How dare you refer to your fiancée's faint as a situation!*

"Yes, sir. I'll tell Sir Reginald you've been delayed." The manservant and family friend looked down his nose at Clotilde as she coyly held onto James. "Would the lady care for anything? Maybe some spirits?"

"Whatever she needs, I'll see to it," James said. He kissed the top of her fair hair, sputtering briefly at the acrid taste of hairspray. "She's mine to take care of."

"Yes, sir," Charles said and turned away, his lip curled in disgust.

James settled Clotilde on the huge bed in her room, propped pillows behind her head, and spread a light blanket over her. "Please, take at least a bit of water. You might be dehydrated."

Wine! Vodka! You idiot. If I'm going to be wed to you by weeks' end, I'm celebrating. "Yes, just a little Evian, please. I think I'll lie down for a bit before making our wedding plans." She sighed deeply and smiled as seductively as she could. She prepared for her next line by imagining a three-way with Randy and André the well-endowed porn star. "Oh, how I am looking forward to being with you. As one."

James bent in for a warm kiss on her full, inviting mouth but was met by a last-minute head turn and a heavily powdered cheek. "Not right now, dear. I'm still faint. Go see to your friend, Sir Reynaldo."

"Sir Reginald," he said, then winced at correcting her. "Reynaldo, Reginald: they sound alike, don't they? I'll be back as soon as I can."

"Oh, don't rush. I'll be napping. When I awake, we can create our short list of guests and plan a simple menu. Oh, this will be so wonderful," she sighed, thinking of André as she rolled onto her side. "Our wedding night…"

***

"Uncle Reginald!" James called out as he approached the open door of his office. "I haven't seen you since I was this high." He held out his hand to shoulder height. "Or maybe shorter. I seemed to be about two years behind all the other lads in growth."

"Maybe in physical growth," the tall good-looking gray-haired gentleman said, "but you were at least that many years ahead of them in intelligence.

James shrugged, humble yet proud at the praise. "It was a gift."

"Was? *Pshaw!* I hope you still have it. It's not as if it disappears with age." Reginald looked at the framed photo on the desk. A glamour shot of Clotilde wearing nothing but a silver fox stole and a pout. 'For my love, C,' was scrawled across the bottom with a broad-tipped black marker. He chuckled. "Still thinks she's a movie star. Has a brief walk-on in a B horror movie and she…"

Reginald could feel the scowl. He looked up and saw the dark eyebrows of his godson's son crowd together. Dumbstruck, he set down his glass of brandy. "Oh, good God Almighty, James. I heard you were considering marriage, but don't tell me…"

Jaws set so tight the muscles twitched, James remained silent at the unexpected and unintentional slur on his fiancée's character from a man he loved and respected.

Seeing the level of tension shoot from zero to toxic, Reginald decided it would be best if he played it cool. "Son, this is a big step. Your father was very dear to me. I know you miss him greatly. Bruce left us too soon. I just wish your grandfather were here to counsel you."

James cleared his throat loudly but didn't say a word.

"By that, I take it he's already tried to talk you out of marriage?" Reginald asked. "Or just out of marriage to Clotilde?"

James rolled his eyes and relaxed, the tension melting at the unique perspective. "You know, I don't know which one it was, if either. I think it was meant to be the generic 'You're too young to wed' speech. Would you believe he said I should take a hiatus for a month or two, go to some tropical area of the world where English wasn't spoken, and just… Well, he said I should screw my eyes out and get it out of my system, that I wasn't in love with

76

Clotilde, I was in lust. In retrospect, I don't know if he would have said the same thing if I was engaged to her, a Swedish princess, or a coal miner's daughter."

"Well, that's one way to look at it. I don't necessarily advocate exposing yourself to a myriad of social diseases and lawsuits, but a few casual liaisons with interesting women wouldn't be a bad idea. That is, if it's not too late. You haven't actually given her a ring or signed a contract, have you?"

James shrugged. "Yes on the ring. I would have given her a bigger one, but she said the one I bought was big enough for now. We did get a marriage license but haven't had it officiated. We...um...were going to do it this weekend. Would you honor me by being a witness?"

"Bu...but... That's so soon! How long have you known her, James? You should be engaged for at least a year."

"When you know it's right, you know it...right?" James asked, a nervous twitch starting in his left eye.

Reginald saw the sign of indecisiveness and insecurity but didn't comment. "We'll see. I'll have my secretary in Edinburgh check my calendar. I just got back from India. At your father's behest, I made some investments for you when you were quite young – still cutting teeth, I believe. We did well. I matched the amount for you with a few rupees of my own. It looks like you're a much richer man today. Now, I was a bit sneaky on this, though. I took it in paper rather than put it in the bank."

Reginald opened his briefcase and pulled out one of at least a half dozen bloated manila envelopes. "I figure it's always nice to have cash on hand for emergencies. You can place it in the bank if you'd like, but then they'd ask questions about where it came from. Did you liquidate stocks or bonds, or... Well, you get the idea."

Reginald took a deep breath and looked up at the large, framed portrait of Lord Anthony Melbourne, an ancestor of the family. He noticed it was cattywampus and possibly open. He nodded to it.

77

"And please, start locking that safe. It looks like a refrigerator door with all those handprints at the bottom from the repeated opening and shutting. Use your desk for frequently accessed items instead of the 'not-so-well-hidden' safe."

"Excuse me?" James asked and looked closer at what he was referring to.

Reginald saw the confusion and realized it was probably too late. Clotilde had not only brainwashed him, but she had slithered into his secret hiding places, already seeking whatever she could find to enrich herself and her slimy friends.

"Here, let me do something for you. Do you know the combination of this safe?"

James shook his head. "It's so old, the locksmith couldn't figure it out. It's evidently custom-built, too. He'd never seen another like it."

"Yes on the former – it's old – but not so much the latter. I have its twin." Reginald picked up all six packets of cash, set them in the safe, and shut the door. He turned the knob, overcoming the start of a protest from James.

"Let's see if this works." Reginald turned the dial to the left six times to reset any old code that was in it. He needed to create a new combination. A birthday or anniversary would be too easy to guess. He looked over and saw James, the pride and joy he wished he had fathered. Except for the brain fart of an obsession with the siren, Clotilde, he was quite the genius.

And there was his inspiration for the numbers. "One to the right, eight to the left, five to the right," Reginald said. He tore off a piece of paper, wrote the numbers out, and handed the slip to James. "Do those numbers mean anything to you, son?"

James looked side to side and grinned. "Well, yes, they do to me. I wouldn't know what they mean to you, though."

"Tell me what they mean to you."

78

"One eighty-five is my IQ." He shrugged then took a deep breath and grinned. "But you knew that, didn't you? You were the one who insisted my intelligence was measured when I was only yay high." James stuck his hand out to shoulder height again.

"Or less," Reginald said, moving the hand down. He reached around and gave James a hearty hug. "Oh, I so wish your grandfather were here. He loves you so much. It's at times like this, just before being wed, you need someone to talk to. He'd even be better to counsel you than your father."

"I do know a bit about life, Uncle. I'm a little too old to be getting the birds and the bees talk from anyone."

"It's not that. You were reading anatomy books instead of comics before you lost your first tooth. No, it's your lack of life experience and knowledge about grift and greed that scares me." Reginald saw James tense. "But you're an adult, and I'm sure you've done your due diligence on her background and criminal file, whether she's filed bankruptcy once or multiple times, or has large judgments against her that are due soon…"

Reginald looked at James for his reaction. He was blinking. He hadn't thought of that. The seed was planted now. Love – or lust – had an odd way of blinding a person. You could explain the logic to a sharp but smitten person all day long, but he wouldn't listen. Sometimes, though, if you set out a pair of glasses, he might pick them up and use them. Hopefully, that's what he'd just done for James.

***

James had taken dinner without her, dining in the kitchen with the help. Clotilde had shunned his company, her door locked and unanswered at his gentle knocks. Hopefully, it was just dehydration, and she wasn't suffering a major malady. It had been a long day of travel and turning in early wasn't a bad idea. He'd be fresh for the morrow.

Soothing sleep evaded him, though. He tossed and turned all night. Horrible nightmares about a white tiger haunted him. The sleek and beautiful tame animal turned on him, suddenly and without warning reaching out and slashing, biting and tearing the hand that had just fed it. The final assault came as the giant cat reared up and went for his head, its long white teeth and deep pink maw approaching in slow motion as he stood helpless, arms at his side. Defenseless. The mouth snapped shut as if spring-loaded, blocking out all light. The loud crunch of his skull as it caved in awakened him.

Gasp! He sat up straight, a cold sweat drenching him. He threw off the covers and looked around, verifying he was alone in the room and there weren't any wild animals present. He realized he was panting and slowed his breath to a shallow, steady pace. *No need to hyperventilate and pass out, Melbourne. It was just a dream. Next time, just say no to cook's triple-layer chocolate torte before going to bed.*

James took a sip of water from the bedside glass and verified the time. "Six a.m. It was just a dream. Bad thoughts, indigestion, whatever. Nothing a nice warm shower won't wash away."

He turned on the shower and grinned. "A nice warm shower with a little personal happy time is in order, I believe. Clotilde may be saving herself but a little spilled seed on my end will make the day brighter. At least for me and anyone who has to deal with me. It's been too long…"

The warm water over his head and shoulders, dribbling down his back, sent tingles down his arms. A little shampoo to the hair whether it needed washed or not softened the water even more. The suds slipped down further as he put one hand against the shower stall, the ever so soft warmth traveling over his balls, making them tighten as his cock grew harder. A few well-practiced strokes, and he was gasping, the image of his fiancée's spread legs enhancing his personal pleasuring. "Ahh."

80

Attitude brightened, James donned his bathrobe and went to the small desk in his room to check emails. Nothing important. He checked the time. Not even seven. A cup of coffee with the crew downstairs, maybe an egg and a piece of toast, and he would edit the short list of people to invite to his wedding. A tingle sped to his loins at the thought of his wedding night. He looked down and patted the bulge in his terrycloth robe. "Not again, you hungry beast."

The thought brought a sudden uneasiness. Could she really be a virgin? If so, he'd have to be gentle. He didn't have experience there, but certainly the books he'd read had some truth in them. Could he go slowly after waiting so long for her?

He wouldn't think anyone her age could still be a virgin, even at her admitted age of twenty-two. By the references to some of the events she'd attended, she had to be nearer his age or even older, maybe thirty. Still, he knew never to question or correct her. How anyone could pout for a week over a simple correction of grammatical use was an enigma. Still, she was 'the one' for him. She had to be the woman destined to be his wife. Right?

Little flutters of uncertainty darted in, squelched by fantasies of bedroom frolics, freedom to enjoy each other's bodies fully. He looked at the time on the computer. He'd been wrapped up in daydreams for half an hour. "A light breakfast and sunshine ought to clear the head."

James dressed and brought his notebook downstairs, refusing the cook's insistence that she feed him at the big table in the dining room. "I'd rather sit in here with you, where there's life, warmth, and the smell of dinner to come," he said.

"You always were my favorite," Cookie said, patting his shoulder. "Well, you and your grandfather. Sir Martin also had a hearty appetite and a kind word."

James chuckled. "Ah, fond memories of stolen pasties."

"The both of you," she said. "You were much more like your grandfather than your father. God rest m'lord Bruce's soul wherever it may be."

"Didn't you hear me call?" Clotilde asked harshly as she stormed in the kitchen. She looked over and saw James sitting at the table and changed her tone. "I rang for tea. I guess there's something wrong with the intercom."

"Oh, that might be," Cookie said. She brought out a tea tray, already set with a cup and pitcher of hot tea. "I thought you'd be wanting some, so I had it ready. Where would you like to be served, ma'am?"

Clotilde subconsciously rolled her eyes, disgusted at the designation, eager to be called 'm'lady.' She pasted on a fake smile and nodded to the table. "I'll take tea with my fiancé," she said, then added with a tinge of snark, "if you don't mind."

Cookie quickly set another place at the staff's table across from James and returned Clotilde's sour remark with a bright smile. "You honor us with your presence, ma'am."

James watched the exchange, proud that his surrogate mother wasn't returning his fiancée's early morning dour attitude. He smiled at Clotilde. "I was just putting together a short list of friends and family I'd like to invite this weekend."

"I've changed my mind, dear," she said, averting his gaze and watching the cook pour tea. "I think it would be best if we wed this afternoon. There's a cruise headed for Greece bright and early tomorrow. I hope you don't mind, but I used the card you gave me to book our stateroom. Just think, sailing to Greece as man and wife..."

"Wait. What? How come? I mean, why the sudden change?"

Clotilde brought out the super pout, adding a brief snivel. "But don't you want to be married to me?"

James put his hand on hers. "Of course, I do. It's just I asked my Uncle Reginald to be our witness. I seriously doubt he can make it this afternoon. He already left for his home in Scotland."

"You can send him pictures, can't you? I'm sure we can hire a photographer last minute."

James pursed his lips, deep in thought, pondering the advice Reginald had given him. What his father or grandfather would have said about this change. His father would be all for it. He had blathered on and on about how wonderful Clotilde was the last time they spoke on the phone. His grandfather…

Sniff, sniff.

"What's wrong, dear?" he asked.

"Don't you want to be married to me?" Clotilde repeated, blotting away invisible tears, hoping her eyes looked red and puffy enough to invoke a major load of guilt.

"Oh, no, no, no," he soothed. "Yes, I'll make a few calls and make sure we have everything in order."

He looked up at Cookie, ready to ask her if Charles was in the house. Her face was white as unbaked meringue, eyes as wide as egg yolks. She returned his gaze and quickly shut her mouth, grimacing into a fake smile. Stunned, wordless, but always there for him.

"Oh, there you are, m'lord," Charles said, walking into the room to break the tension. "Will you be needing my services today? I understand there might be some activity planned."

James gasped in shock at his sudden appearance but composed himself quickly. He could tell by the iron mask Charles was wearing that he'd heard the whole conversation but knew – or believed – it wasn't his place to comment about his employer's snap decision to rush into marriage. "I…I *could* take the Corniche, but for this event, I think it would be best to have an escort, don't you agree?"

"Yes, m'lord. I don't think it would be proper for any man to drive himself to and from his nuptials. I'd be happy to attend you and your..." Charles paused and looked at Clotilde, her eyes squinted in sheer loathing at him. "And your intended."

***

Six hours later

"Thanks for standing in as the witness, Charles," James said. "I'd like to give you..."

Charles set his hand on James's shoulder. "If you're thinking of offering me any kind of compensation for being your friend, please don't. I consider it an honor to be in such high esteem."

James chuckled. "You and I both know it was an act of desperation, but you're right. If I took out all the obligations that went with a marriage ceremony – honoring certain traditions, relations, and connections – I would have chosen you first. Uncle Reginald was asked. He is a great man, and my father's godfather, but you have been a great friend and comfort to me since I can remember. Thanks for always being there for me."

"My honor and privilege. However, I do not think it right that you pack for your voyage on your wedding night. Are you sure there isn't something I can do for you?"

"I always have a bag ready to go at a moment's notice. Anything I don't have such as summer wear, I can pick up onboard or at the first port of call."

Charles nodded, then put out his hand. "Congratulations, sir. I hope all works out for you." He subconsciously ended his sentence too soon, so he started again. "I hope all works out for you and Lady Clotilde."

The apprehension wasn't missed by James. He'd been getting that vibe from the staff all day. Nothing said aloud, but their body language all chorused, "Don't do it!"

Little shivers ran up his spine. Could they be right?

Two more hours later

Was that it? I thought my wedding would be all glitters of happiness, tingles of joy – at least on the inside. Did I make a mistake?

I should have postponed the ceremony as soon as she said her stomach was in turmoil. 'But we're already here.' What a lame excuse. And here I thought, 'What's the rush?' was a valid question. I mean, it's not as if there hasn't been a registrar in that same building for the last three hundred years!

I hope she's right and the fresh sea air will make her feel better. So much for consummating our marriage on our wedding night. I guess I'll have to be my own best friend again and take another extra long shower. I hope I don't run out of hot water this time.

Chapter 8: The Honeymoon Sea Cruise

One week later, at sea

"We can't do that!" Sarah squeaked. "The men will hear us."

"Ah, so they'll ken I'm servin' ye well. Dinna fash, they're decent lads. They have no desire to watch. Ye did say that in yer time, people did that, aye? Watched each other copulating?"

"Yes, I mean no, I mean. It was in movies. Moving pictures, like portraits that moved and talked, but the screens – the canvases – were bigger. Well, some of them were smaller. I mean, can't we just wait until we're at an inn?"

Jody leaned in and rubbed his nose under her ear, tickling her on purpose. "The folks would be a lot closer to us at an inn than out here in the rough. Plus, the mattress is softer here." He patted the plaid-covered leaf pile he'd put together for her. "And probably a lot less buggy."

Sarah squealed as a garter snake slithered across the edge of the covering and into the golden leaves. "Weel, probably fewer snakes at the inn," Jody said. "But the ones out here are naught but the wee fellows that feed on the crawlies and vermin. They willna bother ye." He tickled her in the ribs, making her squirm, then grabbed her round bottom, firm from working the fields alongside him. "Yer too big to swallow."

"What drivel," Clotilde said, shutting the purloined paperback. "The least old Marty could have done was dog-ear the good stuff. Why for God's name can't they figure out how to provide Wi-Fi at sea? Two weeks without porn, watching André…"

Knock. Knock.

"Grrr," she mumbled, then spoke up in a thin, whiny voice, "Yes, dear?"

"Are you okay? Is there anything I can do for you?" James asked.

"Oh, no. There's nothing anyone can do about a nasty case of food poisoning. That is unless you want to sue the ship lines for putting out spoiled lobster." *Cough. Cough.* "Oh, no. I think I'm going to be sick again," Clotilde said, then rolled over and screamed into her pillow.

"I'm going on deck to get some fresh air. Tell the steward to find me if you need anything. I'll be back in an hour to check on you."

"Th...thank you," she stammered, using her self-taught acting skills. "You're so sweet." *And gullible!*

James walked away. Again. Still frustrated. What was he supposed to do? He'd been married for one full week and hadn't had so much as a passionate kiss. Five days of delays for 'female issues' he could understand, but supposedly she was sick from the buffet. No one else on board had so much as indigestion the ship's doctor assured him. Time for another consultation.

James stepped into the tiny anteroom of the doctor's clinic and saw he was the only patient. The nurse told him she'd let her know he was here.

"Dr. Waymire, I hate to disturb you." James looked around the small room. The only place to sit other than the doctor's stool, was on the exam table.

"Please, get comfortable,," the dark-haired beauty said, nodding to the table. Once he was seated, she put her hand on his wrist to check his pulse. "Now, what can I do for you?"

"It's not me. I'm not sick," he protested, trying to pull his hand away.

"I'll check it since you're here. Oh, by the way, how's your wife?"

"That's why I came by. She's been locked in our room, sick for nearly three days. Can you make a house call? Or is that a stateroom call? Either way, I'm getting tired of sleeping on a cot in the gymnasium. I guess that's better than being on deck. I think there's such a thing as too much sea air."

The doctor chuckled at his remark as she felt under his jawline for swollen glands, his forehead for any sign of fever. Suddenly, it registered what he'd said. "Wait. You mean you haven't slept with your wife – I mean, in your own room – for two days?"

James shrugged then winced, brought up short by the kink in his neck.

"Let me check that out." She stood in front of him. "Here, let me get closer." James put his knees apart and she moved right next to the exam table, her cool hands on either side of his neck.

"Your neck muscles are as tight as steel cables. What have you been doing?"

"As I said, finding odd places to sleep the last two nights. For five days before that, I was making do on the floor with a blanket and pillow."

The doctor picked up her clipboard and scanned down the passenger list. Melbourne, James, stateroom. In parentheses was noted British lord – honeymoon. She set it down and said, "Lie down on your belly, please."

"I'm not here for me. I'm fine. I'm worried about my wife." He saw the doctor's scowl and did as he was told. "How's this going to help her?"

"You're my patient, not her. I can make a house call after I try to untangle the knots in your neck and shoulders. I'm surprised you don't have headaches."

James relaxed into her strong fingers, tensing slightly as she pressed on a tight muscle. If only his wife would do this for him. Do anything for him…

"You've made a huge mistake, James. It's not too late to back out. I'm sorry I wasn't there for you," Grandpa said. "But even if I had been, I suspect you wouldn't have listened to me. You always

did have to try it your way first. It's not too late. You can undo this marriage."

The doctor felt him relax completely. Sound asleep.

What kind of woman would kick *him* out of bed? Even a lesbian would give this one a try. Well, maybe not every lady lover, but she sure would. Compassionate, well built from all she could see, probably rich since he was staying in a stateroom, and a member of the House of Lords, to boot? Was that wife of his crazy or mean or both?

She threw a sheet over Lord James Melbourne's dozing form and patted his back in dismissal. It was a slow day. She'd let him rest until she needed the room. Maybe if he slept his head would clear and he'd see he was married to a gold digger. His marital situation wasn't her concern, only the health of his body. It would be best to stay out of it and hope he figured it out himself.

She shut the door behind her and went into the lobby. Still, a waste of a good man.

***

Ding-ding. Ding-ding.

James awoke with a start. It was the lunch – or was that dinner? – bell. He lifted his head and wiped his mouth. He'd been sleeping soundly but for how long and where? He sat up and looked at the wall. The skinless face of a human skull, complete with bug eyes and sinuses, looked out at him, the illustration stark and scary after his vivid dream of his grandfather scolding him. Was the old man in danger? He thought of the message he'd received via the dreamland wire. Hmph. Was *he* in danger?

He appeared to be in a doctor's office. Oh, yeah. He'd come to see the doctor about Clotilde. He must have fallen asleep when she was releasing the tension...

"Oh, shit! I told Clotilde I'd check on her in an hour. She's probably wondering where I am, worried that I'm okay." He rubbed the sleep from his eyes. "Or not."

James walked slowly down the deck, a condemned man to sentencing, in no hurry to find out his fate. She'd put him off on consummating the wedding for a week now. Her first lie – we aren't fully married until we're in international waters – so blatant, he thought he'd lose his cool. Still, he let her think she was right. After all, she did have her 'monthly' to contend with. Maybe that was the real reason, and she didn't want to admit it.

Could she possibly be suffering from morning sickness? That was the doctor's first question on his initial visit to her. "No, we haven't had relations," he told her, a blush rising at the admission. He could see her bite off the remark that it could be someone else's child. At least, Dr. Waymire had a robust sense of decency. He'd thought of it, too. But when? With whom?

Waves of mucky mind garbage weighed him down, disgusting thoughts of all the opportunities she'd had to cheat on him – deceive him, misdirect him, steal from him – since they'd been together. Had he been the biggest sucker in the candy store? Apparently, his subconscious knew it. He'd been so focused on her comfort and happiness, he'd neglected his own self-care. Even a small portion – a decent bed to sleep in – should have been a concern for her. If she truly loved him. Or even had a sliver of respect for him as a human being.

James looked up. He was at their cabin. Did he even want to go in – to confront her with his observations? A seagull flying overhead, calling out its announcement that land was nearby, brought him back to the present. He put his hand on the doorknob and turned. The moment of reckoning.

It was unlocked.

"Oh, there you are, darling," Clotilde called out, all dressed and coifed, ready for dinner at the Captain's table. "Do hurry up and change. You look like you've slept in those clothes. I'm sure Charles packed a suit for you. I do hope you hung it up when we got here. It doesn't seem like we've been on this boat – excuse me, this ship – for a week, does it?"

Clotilde's blathering went on and on; dozens of words spoken but nothing said. Was this better than her quick quips that essentially said, 'Be quiet and leave me alone?' He unbuttoned his shirt, sniffed his armpit, decided a quick deodorant cover-up would have to do, then finished getting dressed. Concentrating on the steps of changing clothes tuned her out and channeled away the negativity of his earlier thoughts. Diverted, but not forgotten.

***

The next day
Piraeus, Greece

"I can only talk a moment, dear Randy. We just got into Port Something-or-other. I can't pronounce these names. No, there was no cell service at sea. Would you believe, I couldn't even get wi-fi? Yes, that's why I didn't send an email. No, darling. I've remained true to you. I didn't sleep with him."

Clotilde giggled. "Not even the innocent kind. The whole time, I had him sleep on the floor or wherever he could find a place. I didn't care. As long as he wasn't in the same bed with me. What? You want me to sleep with him? You mean, have sex with my husband? Oh, no…no…no. Oh, I suppose you're right. It isn't legal if it isn't consummated. Well, there is a big celebration tonight because we made it to Greece. I guess I'll get stinking drunk and let him do it." She paused, imaging André was on board, too, and he wanted her. *Ahem.* "And I'll be thinking of you the whole time."

Clotilde looked up and saw James coming her way. "I have to go, Mumsy. I'm glad you're feeling better. Ta ta. Love and kisses."
Click.

She closed the phone quickly and put it in her purse. "Just checking in with family," she said and kissed him on the cheek.

James saw her flush and knew she was lying. She was uncomfortable and it wasn't the heat.

Clotilde immediately noticed something different about him. He hadn't touched her or kissed her cheek. He didn't seem all needy and clingy, either. He was confident. He had a backbone. A chill went up her spine. Was he on to her? She remembered what Randy just said about sleeping with him. She'd have to do it fast and cement the legal and financial bond or lose it all.

She leaned into James, rubbing her breasts on his arm just below the sleeve of his cotton polo shirt. "How come we haven't consummated our marriage," she whispered. "Don't you want me?"

He pulled back, nearly dumping her as she lost her balance. "What?" he hissed sharply.

Hiding her disgust at him for causing the false step in public, she remembered the six packets of cash she had seen in the safe, the new combination written on a scrap of paper in the medicine cabinet. She wouldn't be able to access the funds if he got mad at her and changed the locks and combination. Plus, she still had to be added as a signer on his bank accounts. Her eyes lit up in anticipation of access to more funds.

"Oh, sweetheart," she said and brought back her sure-fire pout. Her fingertips skimmed across his chest, his nipples hardening beneath her touch. "I was feeling under the weather. You can't fault me for that, can you?"

James noticed faces in the crowd, half the tourists staring, the other half pretending to be disinterested, little smirks hidden behind bowed heads as they fussed with hats, hairdos, or the price tags on the locally produced handbags.

"Come with me, Clotilde," he said, the pronunciation of her name harsh with disgust, a firm hand on her upper arm as he led an exodus away from their fellow shipmates. "Let's go back to our cabin. Whatever you had must be contagious. Now I'm not feeling well."

Out of the corner of his eye, James watched her face transition between shock, rage, and forced humility. A smattering of self-loathing at obeying his direction and allowing herself to be led like a dog was also there. He grinned in satisfaction. Maybe that's all she needed: a man to take charge. Well, he could do that. His smile grew. It might be the most fun he'd had in weeks.

Once they neared their stateroom, Clotilde tensed. That 'moment' was approaching fast. James opened the door and saw housekeeping had already come in. The queen-sized bed was freshly made, a decorative *paquette* of tulle and white ribbon containing pastel butter mints on each pillow.

"Here, dear," Clotilde said, slipping around him to get to the bed. "Let me fix this up for you proper, so you'll be comfortable. I know how queasy my stomach was." She snatched the little parcels of candy and tossed them on the dresser, then quickly rearranged all the pillows into a comfortable nest for one person. "Lie down here and I'll get you a seltzer from the bar – a little spritz of something to settle the stomach. Ginger maybe? I'll ask the bartender. He'll know. You just cozy in and I'll be right back."

And then she was gone.

"She did it to me again," James huffed. "I had control of the situation for a couple minutes and the few hundred yards to get here, then she snatched it right back." He kicked off his shoes and lay back on the pillows, fuming. "Bellyache or not, this is not how a honeymoon is supposed to be."

***

"Give me something to drink," Clotilde grumbled.

"What does your heart desire?" the youthful bartender asked, giving her a flirtatious wink.

"Whatever will get me drunk the fastest." She looked up and saw her reflection in the mirror behind the bar. Scowling, angry, two parallel lines between her eyebrows, wrinkles forming. She forced her face to relax and the 'elevens' faded into oblivion. "Rough day," she said and pouted. "Oh, and my friend has a tummy ache. Just in case I forget, would you give me a takeaway cup of something to soothe it? She'll last until I get back. You wouldn't believe what I've had to put up with – her puking all night. I couldn't get a moment's rest."

The bartender knew who she was. The whole crew was talking about the beauty who was a beast, forcing her newlywed husband to sleep wherever he could find a spot. He set a glass in front of her and poured a double brandy, then held a large, perfect ice cube above it. "On the rocks? It might help it go down a little easier."

Her pout slipped into a grin. He was flirting with her. She still had it. "If you say so…"

Three doubles later, Clotilde looked up, ready to ask for a fourth. "Where'd he go?" she asked the blurry visage of an oversized penguin in front of her.

"His shift was over," the middle-aged woman in a white shirt and black vest said. "Would you like a cup of coffee?"

"Irish coffee?" Clotilde asked. "Nah, I hate whiskey. Slip some of that fancy brandy in it. That's good shtuff," she slurred, then lay her head on the bar.

"I'm sorry, ma'am," the shift relief bartender said, "I can't serve you any more alcohol. Would you like help getting back to your cabin?"

"I'm not no stinkin' ma'am," Clotilde raged. "And I'm not in a cabin. I'm Lady Clotilde and my husband and I are in a stateroom, the biggest one they had available. I should know…"

Her head flopped onto the bar again, slobber slipping out of her mouth. The coolness of the drool awakened her with a start.

"What time is it?" she asked, pushing her hair out of her eyes. "Isn't there a party tonight or something?"

"Yes, ma'am...I mean, Lady Clotilde, there is." The server looked behind her at the clock. "You have about one hour until it starts."

Clotilde grabbed a bar napkin and wiped her mouth. "Which way to the staterooms?"

"Out the door and to your left. Oh, and Jason said you asked for a ginger ale in a to-go cup," she smirked and added, "for your lady friend." She grabbed a paper cup and started to fill it from the well, then stepped back in shock, startled as a hand knocked it away.

"He doesn't need no stinking bellyache cure. He's probably lying about feelin' sick, anyhow. Damn hoity-toity millionaire snob."

Clotilde stumbled out the doorway, wincing at the bright daylight. She grabbed the rail to steady herself and sashayed toward her stateroom, her chin high in pride until her hand hit fresh bird droppings. Babbling and waving her arm with disgust, the drunk and disoriented newlywed blonde wavered to the other side of the promenade and wiped the seagull excrement on a deck chair cushion. She took a moment to compose herself, then proceeded to her destination as if nothing had happened.

Clunk! Clatter!

"Son of female dog!" she screeched as she tried to open the stateroom door. "Damned key."

James awoke with a start at the disturbance. He hadn't meant to fall asleep, but the bed beneath him was the most comfortable place he'd laid in a week.

Clotilde tumbled into the room, arms outstretched, room key in one hand, the other grasping for something to steady herself.

James jumped out of bed and grabbed her around the waist, pulling her backside to him to avoid the key she was now holding like a small sword.

"Oh, are you still here?" she asked with a half grin.

"It's my room, too." James stood her up next to the bed, facing him. One slight push on her shoulder and she was down, feet kicking up, eyes to the ceiling. "You can have the room for the rest of the trip. I'm getting an annulment as soon as I get back. I'm sure I can catch a flight out of Athens. You can finish the cruise by yourself."

"But…but it's our honeymoon!"

"Clotilde, I knew you were dim when we first got together, but I thought there was some good in you. I guess I was the dumb one. You care for you and only you."

"Wait, wait… Please don't throw all this away. I'm…I'm just scared, that's all. You know, about the wedding night part. I'm still a virgin, you know." Clotilde reached out for his hand, her head bowed, hiding her grin of deception, hoping the smell of brandy wasn't as strong to him as it was to her.

Nothing. James didn't say a word and it scared her. Crap. Now she'd have to beg. "Please, give me another chance. Stay with me at least until the end of the cruise. Just one more week. You can have the bed, even if I get as sick as I was again…"

Knock. Knock.

James answered the door. The teen in a crisp white uniform handed him a card. "The captain wanted to make sure you were still eating at his table tonight." The young man looked over at Clotilde, one hand tidying her hair, pretending nothing was amiss. "He heard that someone was ill."

James looked back and saw Clotilde straighten up with excitement, the smile that had first attracted him to her now back in place, the pout gone. "Yes, we'll be there." He pulled a folded bill out of his pocket and slipped it in the young man's hand. "Thanks for checking on us."

Only five minutes late – which was early for Clotilde – they arrived at dinner. James and the captain spoke of the flora in the region and how some of the vineyard grapes on these islands were centuries old. Clotilde nodded and smiled, pretending to eat as she pushed food around on her plate, confining her consumption to alcoholic beverages only.

When the steward started their way offering a second round of after-dinner brandy, James shook his head, heading off the visit. She'd had more than enough. It was apparent to everyone in their section she was plastered. Loud to the point of rudeness, a gutter coarseness and braying laugh had overtaken her former demure manner. Normally, she would only listen to conversations with coy smiles and gentle chuckles, keeping her opinions to herself. Tonight, she had become obnoxious and was embarrassing everyone but herself.

"Excuse me," James said, nodding to the captain and the other couples at his table, "but I think I'd better take my wife back to our room. She seems…" He shrugged one shoulder, letting the reason be tacit. They knew.

"But I don't want to go," Clotilde protested. She held her empty brandy snifter high as a signal, looking around for the steward.

James took the glass out of her hand, set it down, and hoisted her to standing by the elbow. "It's been a pleasure," he said to the guests and turned to leave, his irascible wife trying to squirm out of his hold.

"But I don't want to go," she whined again.

"Too bad," James said, humiliated yet determined to get her out of the spotlight before she either puked, created more of a scene, or both.

97

He ushered her toward their room with only moderate resistance. She had calmed down somewhat after she realized he wasn't going to let her have another drink. At least she had ceased calling out loud remarks to people about their dress or general appearance.

Awkwardly trying to keep her upright while he unlocked the room, they finally made it inside, the spectacle of the British lord and his drunken wife now hidden from others. He set her before the bed, and she sat down hard – the hard part her fault because she'd lost muscle control. He waited for her to recover, then turned to leave.

"Wait!" she called after him.

He turned and glared at her but didn't speak.

She swiped a hand across her mouth, checked her breath, then stood up. "We have some unfinished business," she slurred.

"I think not."

She dropped the sleeve off her shoulder and sauntered toward him. Tripping just before she got to him, she tumbled forward.

"Whoa, there..." By reflex, he caught her. Immediately, the thought occurred to him it would have suited her right to fall and break her nose or chip a tooth. Then again, he'd probably be responsible for plastic surgery or dental work if she did. Or she'd want to sue the cruise company for having wrinkles in their rugs.

Clotilde grimaced at being in his arms but drunk or sober, she knew she had to do it. She'd invested three months in this man. She wanted the money. One roll in the sack, a few fabricated events that would create a scandal, then a high-profile divorce. With the right solicitor, she'd get more than half his worth. *Grin and bear it for one night, woman.*

"I'll be in the gym," James said. "Not that you'll need me for anything."

"James, please don't go," she begged, grabbing his arm as he reached for the door. Sincere for the first time since she spotted him in that restaurant months ago, she added, "I really do need you."

She moved close, shut her eyes, and reached out and grabbed his crotch. "Show me what it feels like to be a woman. A complete woman. Take me."

James gulped. No matter what he thought of her, she had him at a disadvantage. Her grip was strong, and she seemed to know what she was doing. Virgin or not, she wasn't letting go.

"Clotilde…"

His protest was cut off as her other hand pulled his face to hers, her mouth covering his, brandy-flavored kisses deep and probing.

Resistance is futile was his last thought.

They fell into a tangle on the bed, rolling over each other, grasping and clutching, pulling off clothes. Like a dream without continuity – a flash of skin, a scrape of nails, yelps and shrieks, a roar of passion – and then it was over. Cold and clammy, disgusting, and unfulfilling for both of them.

Clotilde dashed from the bed into the bathroom and closed the door. He heard her heaving, sick to her stomach, for real this time.

He bit back the question, "Are you all right." It was plain she wasn't. He lay in bed, the top sheet over his loins, reflecting on what had just happened. *Dummy. She didn't give you anything. Certainly not her virginity. You've consummated a sham marriage. It's legal now. No annulment. No recourse. No love. Dummy. Dummy. Dummy.*

James fell asleep, smothered in self-chastisement, and awoke by himself. He looked around the room and saw her, asleep on the floor in front of the bathroom, wrapped in her thick terrycloth robe, a wadded-up towel as a pillow. He smiled to himself. *Hungover and with a stiff neck from sleeping on the floor. It couldn't happen to a more deserving person.*

***

A long week of 'not tonight, dears,' or 'maybe laters' and their cruise was finished. Despite the uncomfortable certainty that he'd been duped, James gave up on the idea of an annulment. He'd thought briefly of pretending they'd never consummated the marriage. She was so drunk, it shouldn't take much to convince her nothing transpired between them. Maybe if he gave her a few bucks, she'd go away. Nah. She'd claim abandonment, deception, breach of contract, or something. Even a third-rate solicitor could find a way to get money from him with this debacle. It was best to put on a brave face and hope she'd change.

They made it back to London without any major embarrassments and only minor drunkenness on her part. Clotilde didn't spare a moment moving in completely, announcing to all the changes she would make to the Melbourne Manse. It didn't make a difference to her whether the property belonged to James or his grandfather. She had claimed it. It was her residence now and hers to redecorate. James wouldn't let her have full rein but did negotiate down to letting her remodel three bathrooms and one dining room. That much should keep her out of his hair.

Clotilde enjoyed entertaining and had guests over at least every two weeks. They were sumptuous affairs, meant to impress others and get her picture on the society page of the papers. Occasionally at these events, she'd show him affection. Her gentle touches and little kisses on the cheek still titillated him whether she truly felt kindly toward him or not. She loved to ramble on about their perfect marriage and led everyone to believe they had a wonderful time behind closed doors.

Even though he knew they were fake, the physicality of her gestures brought out his animal desires. He usually suppressed them, but a couple of times, he chose not to ignore them. He let the yearnings compound until he was fired up too much to cool down, ready to be man and wife again...and not in name only. He could have taken matters into his own hands and relieved himself with a long shower, but – damn it – she was his wife.

She always found the right – or wrong – words to kill his desire, though. Her scathing diatribes and caustic tone could melt a wax taper. Yes, he finally figured out that she got him worked up just so she could put him down. It was her entertainment, her sport.

Other than the one drunken night on the cruise, she only let him become intimate with her once. It was after she had spent a late evening doing research on her new laptop computer. She never would tell him what she was looking up, but he had the sneaky suspicion she had found a porn site. That night, she made the moves on him. Without knocking, she came into his room and climbed into bed with him, quickly shucking her clothes. She grabbed him and rubbed her bony body all over his, murmuring, 'André, take me now, take me hard.'

That night, it felt like another person had taken over Clotilde's body. Then again, that was probably because she was treating him like another man, this man named André. He didn't care what she called him. He had bruises on his hips the next morning, but a smile that lasted until he came downstairs. Maybe she'd become the seductress again...

When he arrived in the dining room for breakfast, she was gone. Not for another shopping trip, but for a much longer period: she had taken her laptop with her. Not bothering to write a note, she had left a short message with Cookie. 'Tell James Mumsy is gravely ill, and I'll be gone until she's better.'

"Have you ever met her mother?" Charles asked James, stepping into the room and the conversation. He nodded hello to Cookie, then looked back at James. "Perhaps there's a specialist who can heal her malady."

"I don't even know the woman's name," James replied, fully aware of the nuance of his friend's question. "She calls her 'Dear

Mum' or 'Mumsy.' Whenever I ask, she gets emotional and does her babble mixed with tears trick."

Charles spat out his sip of tea at the candid explanation.

Cookie handed him a napkin and said, "James knows what he's doing. He can see right through her, can't you, deary."

"Seeing and knowing what to do are two different things," James said. "Although it does seem to flare up whenever she thinks she deserves a holiday."

"Well," Charles said. "I know it isn't my business, but I have a friend who specializes in getting to the bottom of lost, missing, or mysterious people. Silas Priest. I can ring him up or send him an email and maybe he can find out more about Dear Mumsy."

"That's Dear Mum or Mumsy," Cookie said.

James and Charles laughed at her correction.

"Hey, I'm part Sherlock, too," she said. "My mother always did say I should have been a detective."

"I disagree," James said. "Or maybe you would have been great at that, but then I wouldn't have had the best cook in the Western Hemisphere spoiling me for the past twenty-six years."

***

October 30, 2011

"Hello?" Clotilde pulled the phone away from her ear and looked again to make sure she had dialed correctly.

"Hello? Hello?" she repeated.

"Oh, there it is. Damned mute button was on," Sept said. "Hey, it's yer nickel. Whatcha want?"

"This is your, ahem, friend, Lady C. Remember me?"

"Are you that broad with the funny name that sent me two hundred bucks a couple months ago? 'Cause if you are, I need more money. That ran out three weeks past." Sept held the phone away from his ear, then hit another button. "Can you hear me now? I think it's supposed to be on speakerphone."

"Yes, yes, I can hear you. I'll send you more money but first, you must go to the Gillis Courthouse – or whatever it's called – and see if you can find that little man with a map. Take it from him and call me back at this number. This is a new phone number, so don't call the other one."

"Hello? Hello?" Sept said. "Oh, yeah. I remember now. You have that thing goin' on with the treasure map what's needs the key. You say it's gonna be around on Halloween, but you don't know what year, right? See, I got a good membery."

"That's memory, Pa," Eight said.

"Shut yer piehole or I'll shut it fer you," Sept said. "No, not you, Lady. It's my idiot son. Well, actually, he's the smart one. The other one's the idiot. Yeah, I know it's none of yer business. We'll cut ye a good deal. Ye send the money today and we'll look both today and tomorrow. Sound good to ye? Okay. Now, tell me that secret name again. I couldn't remember it last time. Okay. I'll say it out loud and you boys try and remember it, too. Cloe Til Duh. Got it, boys?"

Eight and Niner repeated, "Cloe Til Duh, Cloe Til Duh."

"Yeah, we got it, Lady. Here's hopin' we'll have good news fer ye today or tomorrow. Now, don't ferget the money like ye did last time. I got bills to pay, ye know. Yeah, bye fer now."

"Hey, Pa," Niner said. "We ain't got no bills 'cause with fast hands like ours, we don't buy nuthin'. At least, not much."

"Dummy, we buy beer and gas. And if we're goin' to the Guillyford Courthouse place, we're gonna need gas. Geez, that lady's sure dumb, callin' it the Gillis Courthouse."

***

Two days later

"Hey, Pa," Eight said. "Don't I look like one of them andy-sister type persons?"

103

"That's ancestor," Niner said, then ducked, expecting another blow for correcting his elder.

"Yeah, that's what I said. Anyhow, Pa, I walked around lookin' like one of those other folks workin' the crowds at the Guilford Courthouse, and I didn't see no little man, with or without a map. There was lots of little kids, and one really short old lady, but she hit me with her umbrella when I tried checkin' her out, sayin' she didn't have no map."

Sept tipped back the beer bottle, sucking down the last drop, then tossed it in the back of the van with the other empties. "No problem. We still have a few bucks left. It's a good thing Lady C sent the money right away this time. Come on. Let's go see what other excitement we can scare up. You put on your outfit, too, Niner. Maybe the two of you can do some entertainin' – sing a song or somethin' – and folks will throw coins or dollars at ye."

"I'd rather have them throw dollars," Eight said, "'cause coins can hurt and paper money don't."

"'Sides, dollars are worth more." Niner paused and asked, "Right?"

"Idiot! Depends on the number."

Chapter 9: Billy the Cop

Greensboro, NC
September 2011

"Oh, I'm so glad they have one of these!" Leah squealed, then clenched her mouth shut. *Don't go braying like a jack ass. They'll figure you out for themselves soon enough after they get to know you.*

Leah walked around the barbecue grill in the common area of the fourplex apartment buildings, stifling the urge to jump up and down with glee. *Worth a trip to the store just for a steak.* She looked back at the swimming pool, empty except for a forgotten beach ball dancing around the water. *And I can even grill in my bathing suit!*

She hurried to her apartment, doffed her scrubs and tossed them onto the heap next to the laundry basket, then grabbed her yellow two-piece. She caught a glimpse of herself in the bathroom mirror and realized how naked she looked. She rummaged through the discarded clothes, found a once-worn sundress, sniffed it, then pulled it on over her head. "No stains and it still smells like fabric softener. It'll do."

One more glance at her reflection and she pulled the clips out of the tight bun on top of her head. A quick shake and her hair fell to her shoulders. "Too hot," she said, then bent over and pulled it into a ponytail. "Just right."

Leah grabbed her keys and debit card, then slipped on her flipflops and was out the door, ready to find a T-bone or ribeye steak on sale, whichever looked best for the price. "Oh, and a bottle of red wine."

Fifteen minutes later, she was back to her new home. She had attracted a few stares at the big box store, but those were from gray-haired old ladies. *Probably jealous because they weren't brave enough to go out in public wearing so little when it was so blasted hot. That adage really is right. Arizona: it's a dry heat. There I could handle a hundred and ten degrees and three percent humidity. North Carolina's ninety degrees and ninety percent is totally miserable!*

She took the ribeye steak out of the plastic container and rinsed it in cold water as her dad had taught her, then plopped it on a big plate. After a few sprinkles of steak house seasoning, a judicious amount of stabbing with a fork to push the herbs into the meat and break up the fibers, and flipping it over to do the same to the other side, then prepping was finished. "Tastiest, most tender steaks available anywhere."

She carried the prepared meat, a fork, and a glass of wine to the door, then realized she didn't know the law about drinking in public in Greensboro. She set down her drink on the counter and continued out, her keys jangling on the purple coiled bracelet on her wrist.

At the grill, she noticed a little shelf at the side of the barbecue to set a plate. "All right," she said aloud, glad to unload. "Now, where are you, little clicker?" She walked around the grill three times, lifted the plate twice to look for the igniter – even though she knew there was no possible way it would be located there – then got on her hands and knees and looked up, beneath the metal box.

"Is there something wrong?" a man asked.

Startled, Leah scrambled up from her crouched position to see a very handsome, dark-haired man wearing nothing but a huge smile and a pair of Hawaiian-print shorts. "Um, I was looking for the striker. I think that's what you call it. I mean, that's what we call them in Arizona. You know what I mean, the little button you push to get the fire lit? If not, I guess I'll have to go back to my apartment and see if I have any matches. Damn! I mean, dang. I know I don't. I don't even have a lighter."

"Neither would help you," the man said, his smile widening, eyes twinkling.

"Why not?" Leah asked indignantly, scathing at his arrogance.

He saw the glare and backed his attitude down to a grin with a shrug of apology. "It's not propane."

"Huh?"

"Or butane or gas of any kind. It's a charcoal grill. It's a 'bring your own briquettes' steel container."

"Oh, crap!" Leah huffed, glad that she'd bit back the first expletive that came to mind. "The meat's ready to go and now I'll have to throw it in a frying pan. Damn!"

"Not the same, huh?" he said.

"Not even close," she grumbled and looked up. "Hey... Do you happen to have any charcoal on hand? I'll share if you do?"

"Share that big steak in exchange for a few cubes of burnt wood? Sounds like a bargain to me," he said.

"Can you bring them out before someone else comes by to claim the grill, though?"

"Guard it with your life, would you?" he asked with a wink. "I'll be right back."

Two minutes later, he returned to the grassy commons with a spring to his step, a bag of charcoal, a long-nosed lighter, and veggies on a stick precariously balanced on a plate. He let Leah help unload his bounty, set the briquettes in place, then torched the fire. He stuck out his hand to her. "Oh, and I'm Billy Burke, your neighbor."

"Leah Madigan," she said and shook his hand. "Might as well wait for the charcoals to get hot." She picked up the beach blanket at her feet, unfolded it, and spread it out to its full width. "Have a seat down here where it's cool. There's room for both of us."

Billy started to sit down then stopped suddenly, eyes wide. "Oh, wait. Here, I ran out of hands." He took a can of beer out of his back pocket and gave it to her, then grabbed another one from the other side. "They shouldn't be too warm. They were only back there for a couple minutes."

Leah popped the top and slugged back a cool one. "Ah, just right. I guess it's okay to drink then?"

"Private property, not operating a moving vehicle," he looked her up and down appraisingly, "not underage… Yeah, I'd say you're safe."

"I bought a bottle of wine to go with dinner, but you're right. When you're grilling, beer's just better."

The two chitchatted for a few minutes, then Billy looked back and saw the ashy-white frosting on the coals. "Time to throw on the meat," he said. "Do you want the honors?"

Leah finished her sip. "Nope. I did the prep. Go for it. I'm comfy."

He slapped his knees then sprang up in one smooth move, his shorts slipping down just enough to show a butt dimple.

Ooh. So cute! I haven't seen one of those in forever…give or take a month.

Billy set the steak over the hottest part of the grill, then looked at his watch. "Five minutes, then time to flip. Unless, of course, you're one of those who wants her meat well done."

"Of course, I want my meat well done," Leah said, then giggled. "My steaks, on the other hand, I'd rather have medium rare. I don't want it to moo at me; pink and juicy is just right."

"Ah, a smart one on both counts." Billy sipped his beer, then scowled and tipped his head back as far as he could, trying for one last dribble.

"All gone?" Leah asked. When he nodded and frowned, she said, "I have that wine, but I don't think mixing beer and wine is a good thing. Unless you like hangovers and puking your guts out the next morning."

"I'm good. I have two more if we feel like having one with our meal. No reason to go nuts."

"True," Leah said, then lay back on the blanket. "This is so different from Arizona. Yes, we have grass in a few places. Not many, though, because of water restrictions. Still, this feels different. The blades are just fatter, juicier. And the ground underneath isn't so hard."

Billy wiggled into the blanket playfully then looked over at her. "I saw you moving in the other day," he said. "I was just waking up when I noticed you walking by with a tote. By the time I was dressed, you were gone. I guess you got most of it moved in while I was asleep. Oh, I work third shift, by the way." He propped himself up on one elbow. "And I'm not a vampire, either."

Leah chuckled. "Well, let's hope not. Stocker?"

"Stalker? Me? Nope. Why would I do that?"

"Um, grocery stores, department stores, you know. They have to replenish... Oh! You thought I meant s-t-a-l-k-e-r," Leah said and laughed.

"No, I'm not either kind. I do stalk stalkers, though," he said, eyebrows raised mischievously.

Leah's face fell and he quickly explained, "I'm a cop. A detective. You know, to protect and to serve."

"Oh, yeah..." She looked up at the grill and saw the steak's juices dripping onto the coals, flaring up. "When are you supposed to put on those whatcha-callits?"

"The shish kabobs?" He reached up and grabbed one. "I was all set to grill these tonight," he said, waving the pepper, tomato, and onion kabob like a sword, "but I didn't have any meat. I thought about going vegetarian for a day, but I really wasn't ready to take the plunge. I'm a carnivore by choice," he said and added a comical snarl.

"You're too cute," Leah said with a giggle, then realized she was flirting. *Ah, what the hell. I won't push a good-looking man away, even if he's a neighbor. I won't live here forever, and neither will he if things don't work out.*

Billy heard the coy tone of her voice and a shiver ran up his back. *No, no, no! Don't encourage her!*

Leah watched Billy's face fall at her awkward, subconscious flirt. "Sorry. I know that sounded like I was putting the moves on you. I wasn't. I mean, I'm not." She snorted in frustration and stood up. "I mean, I'll check the steak."

Billy got up from the beach blanket and despite her obvious uneasiness, stood next to her at the grill. "Don't worry about it," he said, then leaned close and whispered in her ear, "I'm gay."

"Oh, thank God," Leah said, then realized how loud she'd said it. "I mean, I'm sorry."

"Why? I'm not."

Leah's face bloomed scarlet, and it wasn't from the late afternoon sun. "I really don't know what I'm doing here, what to say," she babbled, grappling with the tongs, lifting the steak by one edge, then setting it down again.

"Fixing a meal with your neighbor, your new friend maybe?" Billy gently took the tongs from her. "Don't worry. I won't break or fall apart as long as you don't fold, spindle, or mutilate me."

Leah laughed and snorted at his lame joke, then set the tongs down. "You'd better check the meat. I don't know how you like yours."

"Ooh. So, we're best friends now? You're all the way up to asking me how I like my meat?" He wiggled his hips.

"No, no, no!" she answered, still laughing. "I mean, yes on the best friends, no, I don't want details on your sex life."

He gave her a quick kiss on the cheek and picked up the tongs. "I never had a sister, but if I had, I'd want her to be like you."

110

"Back at ya but as a brother. I was an only child. Or as I called it, a lonely child."

Billy looked at the steak then grabbed a sharp knife and cut into it, checking how rare it was. "Just right." He set it on the side of the grill that wasn't so hot and moved the kabobs over for a final searing.

"I grew up in an orphanage," he said, somberness replacing the hilarity they'd both shared. "Not so much as a foster home for a weekend." He shrugged. "I'm not complaining. It wasn't bad. I had lots of brothers that way. The house mother was cool, too. I've had loads of friends over the years but never anyone close enough to even suggest becoming family."

Leah stepped near him, put her arm around his waist, and gave him a quick tug close to her. "Wow. This feels great. Holding a guy and not worrying about whether he thinks I'm hitting on him, or if he's going to hit on me because I gave him a friendly hug. Is this what family feels like? I didn't have cousins, either."

"Same here. I will say," he snuggled close to her, side to side, then set his head on her shoulder awkwardly, purring like a cat, "it feels good."

Leah kissed his forehead quickly, then pushed his head back up and grabbed the tongs. "Come on. Let's go sit by the pool and eat. If someone tries to arrest us for breaking apartment rules, I'll just tell them I've got a cop on my side."

"Pool rules like no eating on pool premises were meant to be broken. City and state laws, not so much. Or at least, I wouldn't have a job if that were the case."

"Well, I'm sure you're good at what you do, Detective Billy Burke. Let's just hope I never need your services."

***

One month later

111

Billy took the book. "My turn to read," he said, then propped his pillows up higher, sharing his king-sized bed with her so they could take turns with the story. He took a deep breath and began,

"His thumb stroked the side of his lover's face. "It looks like you cut yourself shaving this morning. Would you like me to try my hand? It might be easier," he cooed and leaned in to kiss Giorgio's full bottom lip.

"Only if I can service you after, mi amor," his dark-haired lover replied.

"Oh, and how I love how you service me," Julian said. "Come, let's finish the bottle of wine, then break in that new mattress I shipped from England.

Chapter Twelve..."

"Crap!"

"What's wrong, Billy?" Leah giggled. "You don't like it when Lisa leaves love scenes to the imagination?"

"Damned straight," he said, then pulled his quilt up over his midsection. "I mean…"

Leah glanced down as he reorganized the bedding and smirked. "Hey, women get wound up the same way. Sort of." She giggled. "It's just not as noticeable."

Billy looked at her chest and she self-consciously covered her breasts, her nipples rigid. "Well, maybe a couple of little things show it, but cold weather and fear can do the same thing."

Billy snorted. "Just the opposite effect on a guy when he's scared or freezing."

"So, did I tell you?" Leah said, quickly changing the subject before they both got more frustrated.

"Probably not. What?" Billy offered her another chocolate and she shook her head.

"There's another *Lost* book coming out next month. Or maybe it's two months. I swear, they tease readers, saying it's only a month, then another, and then another. Next thing you know, it's been a year. Screw it."

"Yeah, you say screw it now, but I'll bet this last bonbon that you start rereading *Lost* before the next one's available."

"Pbbt! I'll probably have the whole series reread by the time it gets out."

Crack! Rumble, rumble…

Leah tumbled into Billy's arms and buried her head in his naked chest. He patted her shoulder then kissed the top of her head. "It's nothing to be afraid of. By the elapsed time between the flash and the thunder, I'd say it's a mile away, at least. Besides, I've never heard of anyone getting struck by lightning while in bed and under the covers."

Crack-Crack! Rumble, rumble…

Billy flinched, not expecting two strikes at the same time.

"Are you okay?" Leah asked, giggling. "Do you want *me* to hold you?"

"Yes, I mean, no. I mean, only if you want to."

"Are you alright?" Leah asked, sitting up so she could cuddle him. She pulled him close and held him like a scared puppy. "I've never seen you like this."

Billy looked up at her and forced a pout to cover his grin. "But we've only known each other a month. There's lots of me you haven't seen."

"I've seen more than a casual friend should see, Billy Burke. You really need to wear clothes occasionally."

"I do," he said. "Every time I'm in public, I keep everything covered that won't get me arrested for indecent exposure. Because you don't knock when you come in doesn't mean I should wear pants 'just in case.'"

"Yeah, well, when I know you're supposed to be asleep and I only need to borrow cream or coffee, I'm not going to wake you for that."

"Then you'll have to deal with it. I mean, you are a nurse. It's nothing you haven't seen before. Last I heard, all men had one."

"And a few women, too, if they found the right website," Leah said and giggled. "But we don't want to talk about *that!*"

"Okay. You can hold me if you insist..." He laughed, then snuggled down further under the fluffy quilt and under her arm. "By the way, it's your turn to read."

"Just a sec." Leah reached across him and grabbed her water bottle from the nightstand. She took a sip, then set it back. "Is this weird? You know, having slumber parties?"

"Slumber parties with just two people? Yeah. Probably. Slumber parties with only two people of different genders who aren't interested in each other sexually? That's called a sleepover, darlin'. You'd do it with another female, wouldn't you?"

"Well, yeah..."

"So, I'm your best girlfriend," Billy shrugged. "That's the main difference between men and women."

"What is?" Leah asked.

"Women make everything so complicated. Men don't. It is what it is. That's that. Now, read the damned book. And skip to one of your dog-eared pages. I don't want to hear some long-winded proclamation. Get to the good stuff!"

"Gotcha."

"They lay side by side on his plaid, his bare buttocks a shining moon on the ground, as round and gleaming white as the orb in the sky. She lifted onto one elbow and ran one finger down his spine, the goose flesh racing, rising inches ahead of her stroke. "Do you like that?" she asked.

"I'd like it more if I were on my back and yer aim was a little lower. Care to give it a try?"

"After I get more comfortable," Sarah said, reaching for her laces.

Jody turned onto his side to watch. "Do ye need a hand?"

"Not really. I can do it myself this time. I want you to do a little priming while strip. I'll watch you touch yourself as I get naked. Did you know that when I come from, they have shows for men – public ones – where women remove their garments one at a time, doffing them in time to the music? Not so much real music but sultry sounds."

Sarah stood up slowly, swaying to the rhythms in her head, wondering if she could follow through with the brazen display. The chance was slim there'd be anyone in these woods to see her. It was harvest time. Most men were busy, gleaning the fields or repairing their equipment, and didn't take time for their women.

"Da da da da, BOOM!" Sarah sang, verbalizing the last note several decibels louder, her hip punching a hole in the air to the side of it. She saw Jody's head jerk back as if he'd been struck on the chin.

"Doo te doo te doo, BOOM!" she sang out anew, this time dropping her blouse over her naked shoulder.

"Do you want me to continue, or do you want to help me undress?"

Jody gulped, then cupped his balls. "Oh, yer doin' a great job there, wife of mine. Keep it up and I'll try to do the same," he said, stroking the length of his shaft.

Sarah swiveled her hips then leaned forward, one breast falling from her loosened corset. "Just remember to save some for me."

Leah looked down at Billy. He had one hand under his chin, the other under the cover, a cherubic and innocent smile on his face. She reached across and set the book on the nightstand. "Someone sure missed out at having you for a son," she said. "Night, night, sweetheart. Sweet dreams."

Chapter 10: A Good Book

January 10, 2012
Fairbanks, Alaska

"What a lame gift. A fifty-dollar gift certificate to Sprawl-Mart. I should have thought of something else…or at least doubled it." Dani set the receipt back in the shoebox with the other receipts marked 'Personal 2011,' then grabbed another fistful of folded and crumpled paper slips from the large bag marked '2011 Receipts.'

"Maybe next year I'll start a new accounting system," she said. "Hmph. This is next year as far as taxes go." She looked at the cluttered counter, debated on whether she should clean house first, then saw the bag of gallon-sized plastic storage bags she hadn't put away the night before.

"How about a little of both?" She set the box of bags on the table, then rummaged through the 'everything drawer' and found it. One of the dozen purple markers leftover from the gag gift Leah's dad had given her for her twenty-first birthday.

She smiled in recollection. She and Leroy may have had a less than ideal marriage, but one thing was certain: his love for his daughter. Twenty-four years ago, they had married a scant five days after she found out she was pregnant. The two of them spun in different business and social orbits but one fact was undeniable: he was devoted to his one and only child. He even worked from home for a year so he could spend more time with his little sweetheart.

Leroy had teased Leah about the color purple since she could talk. After she realized what colors were, she was always on the lookout. 'Puh-pul' she called whenever she saw anything that color. It was a running gag that only stopped when he died.

One of his last teases was on her twenty-first birthday. He had given her a box gift wrapped with shiny lavender paper, a bright purple bow tied on top with a sprig of silk lilac blossoms. "Purple enough for you?" he asked, a twinkle in his eyes.

"Yup. At least on the outside. Let me check what's inside before I answer."

Leah carefully pulled at the tape, trying not to tear the foil paper. "Ah, to heck with it," she said and tore into it like a three-year-old.

Inside was a pack of twelve dark purple markers, packed in shredded white paper. She looked at her father, one eyebrow raised. "Ho-kay… Am I missing something?"

"I thought these were easier to carry around than buckets of paint. One of these days, you're going to move away from this desert heat and start a new life somewhere else. I'm pretty sure you'll want to decorate in your favorite color. These will give you a head start. Oh, and this is a treasure hunt, too. Dig around in the packing paper. There's something else in there you might find useful in your new life."

"Dad," she said, setting the box on her lap. "I'll never leave you, you know that."

"Well, you and I both know I'm going to be leaving you soon. This damned cancer just won't let go. I'm tired of fighting it. No more chemo. Promise me you won't stick around this place after I'm gone. Your mother had the right idea, getting away from the desert. She may have gone a little overboard in settling in Alaska," he said, looking up at his ex-wife and winking. "But that nursing degree you'll be getting soon will open doors for you all over the world."

He paused, swished a grimace back and forth, then added. "Maybe all over the world, but I suggest you stay here in the good old USA. Politics may seem iffy at times, but you're safe here. Plus, you already speak the language."

Leah chuckled. "All I need is the Spanish I already have," she said as she bent over the box, pushing through the repurposed shredded computer paper.

"Whoa. Is this what I think it is?" She picked up the key fob and saw the logo. "A Toyota? Mine?"

"Yeah, well, what am I going to spend my savings on? I sure as hell don't want the hospitals getting all that's left after the insurance pays out. Nah, even if I weren't trying to keep money out of their hands, I'd want you to have something special for your twenty-first birthday. Come on. Give your old man a push into the parking lot. I'll bet you spot it right away."

Dani grinned in recall. She had come back to Arizona for Leah's milestone birthday and been an accessory in the car's acquisition. Leroy's heart was huge, but his body was barely functional. She was more than happy to pick up and deliver the birthday gift to trump all others: a new Prius, as purple as a special-order paint could get.

"Oh, my!" Leah gasped, her hands grasping the handles of the wheelchair as her knees buckled. "I'm glad I had this to hold onto," she said, then bent over her father's shoulder to kiss him on the cheek.

"So, you think that one's yours?" he asked, turning around in his seat to see her face.

She saw his awkward position and came around to kneel in front of him. "There can't be another father in the world as caring as you, Dad."

"And as creative," Dani added, then clenched her jaws, making sure she didn't ruin the moment for daddy and daughter.

Dani saw Leah frown momentarily at the intrusion, then take a deep breath, making a conscious effort to relax. Still bitter.

How long had Leah held a grudge against her? That was easy. It started when she and Leroy sat her down after high school graduation and told her they were getting a divorce. Dani shook her head. There never would have been a good time to separate. Should they have ever married in the first place? Who knows?

"Stop that 'coulda, shoulda, woulda' crap, Danielle. It's not as if you and Leroy were the only couple in the world to have split up. When she grows up and has a few relationships of her own, she'll understand. In the meantime, be glad she still talks to you."

Dani grabbed a plastic bag and wrote '2012 Business Deductions' across the white label, then picked up another one and wrote '2012 Personal Stuff' on it. "Hey, it's a start," she said in mock defense, then picked up the book that was still on the credenza next to the tackily decorated miniature plastic and foil Christmas tree.

"Lost by Lisa Sinclaire," she read. She looked inside the book for at least the twentieth time since she'd opened the present on Christmas Eve. She took out the handmade gift tag and read it again. 'Enjoy the story about the most perfect man in the world. Love, Leah.'

"Stop distracting yourself. At least get your taxes started before you kick back and read a book. Plus, you have three new websites to build and half a dozen more to update. Pick one or the other, but you don't have the luxury of time to read." She looked outside the winter-frosted window and glared at the bleak darkness of the mid-morning hour. "At least until it's bedtime or you have all the websites taken care of, whichever comes first."

Dani set the book back down and went to work. Using the creative side of her mind first, she switched back and forth between the three websites until she realized she was mixing up the themes. "Crap. Your brain is fried. Eat lunch and take a break. Crossdressing in websites doesn't work. Stop trying to multitask. You need to keep the borough, author, and e-store sites separate or you'll never get another contract from anyone."

Her stomach rumbled again. "I guess that's what true hunger feels like. It's been a while." She rummaged through the

119

refrigerator for the fastest and easiest dinner: leftovers. She removed the foil from a covered disposable pan and gagged. The two-week-old lasagna she kept forgetting to eat was now a biology project, covered with fuzzy bumps of green and blue mold. She tossed it in the sink, then started on a crusade: get rid of any food over two days old or that she wasn't going to eat for dinner.

By the time she was done with the top shelf, she had filled the kitchen garbage can, even tossing the food-filled reusable plastic containers. "I'm not gonna even look in those much less wash them. I'd rather buy more."

When she was done, the refrigerator only had milk, butter, and a box of baking soda. All that work, and she still hadn't found anything to eat.

"Got distracted again, eh? Yeah, well, you've been wanting to do that for two months, at least." She filled a big bowl with dry cereal, opened a snack-size container of peaches, drank its juice, dumped the dark-yellow bits on top of the frosted corn flakes, and covered the dinner-dessert combination with a hefty slug of milk.

"Ah, I feel like I'm twenty again," she sighed, looking at her late lunch, flashing back to her college days. "Cup of soup, salad, or cereal. Maybe I ought to go back to that regimen. At least I could fit in single-digit-sized pants."

The cereal was so good, she decided to have a second helping, this one without the fruit. A smaller pile of cereal and double dash of milk, and getting back to work was delayed another five minutes.

Picking up the bowl, she slurped down the last extra sugary sweet sips of milk. "I think maybe a little lie down is needed before creating shopping categories for the Big Bad Boys' Toys site. How they ever got a name like that, I'll never know." She paused and giggled. "Yeah, I thought of that one, didn't I? And here I thought I was being sarcastic when I suggested it."

Dani picked up the paperback and reread the back cover for the umpteenth time. 'An accidental trip through the massive pillars of a Scottish Stonehenge thrust a British nurse back to eighteenth-century Scotland and into the arms of a young redhaired rogue. *LOST* – a timeless tale of lovers from two centuries, their passion so great, even time couldn't part them – will have you gasping, yearning for more. Share in their intimacy, their wanton desires, craving each other's bodies and souls on a level never before reached in literary romance.'

"Hmph. Pretty sure of yourself, aren't you, Lisa Sinclaire? Okay, I'll try to get into it again." Tossing the throw pillows to one end, she grabbed an afghan from the stack in the wicker basket and arranged a cozy reading nook on the couch.

"Here's hoping I can get past the first three pages this time. Maybe a few moments of romance will clear this brain fog." She set the book on the floor next to her, then settled in. After throwing the afghan over her legs and feet, she looked down, huffed in frustration, then reshuffled the pillows so her neck was high enough to see over her boobs. Finally cozied up, she reached for the book.

"Damn! Where'd you go?" She leaned further over the side of the sofa and fumbled for the elusive paperback. She tagged it with her fingertip but couldn't grasp it and accidentally knocked it further under the couch. "Damn, damn, double damn! Ah, hell. I forgot my reading glasses, anyhow."

Dani pulled the afghan up over her shoulders, turned on her side, and promptly fell asleep.

'Where am I? This isn't an Alaskan forest and certainly isn't the Arizona desert. How did I get here?'

Ah-ooh! Ah-ooh!

'A wolf? Ah, shit! I'd better get out of here! Over there, that looks like a trail. Man, where'd I get so much energy? I feel like a teenager again. I could do this all day.'

Dani shifted on the couch, the movement causing her to rouse. Quickly holding onto her dream, she scooted back, hoping the vibrant memory and sensation of being her youthful self again would return.

'Ahh... I'm back. Oh, crap. It's cold and starting to snow. At least, I'm wearing a flannel shirt. I'd better find protection fast. No telling how much is going to fall...or how long I'll be here. Maybe I can build a shelter. Hmph! Maybe if I had an ax or saw. Even a knife would help.'

Ah-ooh! Ah-ooh! Yip, yip, yip. Wimper...

'That sounds more like a dog than a wolf. Maybe he's tangled in a barbed-wire fence or a wild-animal trap. Dang. I'd want someone to help my dog if he was trapped. If I had a dog...

Ring! Ring! Ring!

"Son of a bitch!" Dani snarled and bolted upright on the couch, roused from her recurring dream by the unknown-caller ringtone on her phone. All her contacts had personalized tones, so she could ignore spam calls. "Hello?"

"Congratulations! Your name has been..."

Click.

"Damned robocalls." She resisted the urge to smack the phone on the counter, giving the caller an earful. It wouldn't have worked since there wasn't a real person on the other end. Plus, the screen on her classic cell was one 'oops' away from being garbage. Not enough in the budget to get a new one, though.

She looked over at her desk, scattered with sticky notes, sample flyers, and photos to be scanned. "One site at a time, at least for today. Get it done and billed, then maybe you can afford a new phone." She chuckled. "At least, it's not just me. Leah's was as bad as mine last time I saw her. Maybe she can recommend..."

Hmph! Dani grunted then went back to work. "She has her own life now. Don't make decisions based on what she would, could, or should do. Okay. Now, let's make separate categories for wearables, consumables, and durable goods," she mumbled as she bent to work.

The kindergarten graduation family picture on the refrigerator seemed to be calling to her. She looked at it and shook her head. "They either don't grow up fast enough, or they grow up too soon. Too bad I can't have a do over. There's so much I'd do differently…"

Chapter 11: Truth or Dare

January 2012

Head bowed, she glanced sideways, hoping to see his reaction. Was he truly mad at her for speaking her mind, or was he only trying to impress his kinsmen? His mother had been opinionated, too. That was in her favor. A strong-willed woman could only be loved by a man not threatened by her, his uncle had said. On his deathbed, he admitted he'd yearned for her, too. His sire – Jody's grandfather – had counseled him against wooing her. He said she was too spirited and would be hard to manage. Best to leave her to a swineherd or cotter where her energies could be channeled into useful labor. Not pursuing her had been his greatest mistake, he pined. His brother hadn't listened to their father and wound up with a wonderful wife.

"Are ye looking fer something in particular or jest wonderin' if I'm still alive?" Jody asked, a remorseful half-grin brightening his once scowling face. "I'll tell ye now, I'm breathin' jest fine. However, I am a bit sore in the largesse."

"Large ass?"

"Nae. Largesse. Somethin' given with graciousness, not expectin' anythin' in return. I meant no disrespect, wife," he said, his hand out, beckoning to her...

At the sight of his co-workers exiting the elevator, KK closed the paperback and returned it to the pocket of his scrubs. "Okay, no excuses, all right?" he said rather than asked. "This is the first night we've all had free since..." He pinched his goatee in thought.

"Since we weren't two nurses short," Leah said.

"Yeah, what he said," JJ echoed. "No excuses." She pulled the clip out of her hair, twisted it up again, and put it back. "Man, I'd say I'm gonna miss the extra money for more shifts, but I think

Uncle Sam took all but ten percent of my overtime pay. Between that and my poor feet screaming at me at the end of the day, it was almost enough to make me give up and go on welfare. Nah, not really. But I swear, I'd quit this job and go somewhere else if I didn't think the next place would be just as rough. Students can't graduate fast enough to fill nursing positions."

"That's because people are living longer," Leah said.

"So, what are we supposed to do? Shut off medical attention once someone hits sixty?" KK asked, taking off his ID and stuffing it in his front pocket.

"Ew! No. That'd mean my nana wouldn't be here," JJ said.

Leah looked at her and chuckled. "Or my mother."

Her co-workers stared at her bug-eyed. She replied to their unspoken question. "Hey, I was a surprise baby, but on the other end of the fertility spectrum. What's so unusual about that?"

"I was brought up by my nana," JJ said, "so that's probably why you and I get along so well – both brought up by older women. Yeah, I think I'll start saying I don't want to have kids until I'm in my later thirties, maybe forty, because I want to be more mature like my nana."

KK snickered at her. "Come on, tell the truth. You're not hitched or breedin' because there's not a man alive who's up to your impossible standards."

JJ zeroed in on him with a devilish smile and hugged him around his broad shoulders. "Yes there is, but he's gay."

"Ew! Babies," he groused. "They'd have to pay me to clean up the muck that comes out of those little behinds."

"Dawdle if you want, but I'm leaving," Leah said. "I want to take a shower and clean up my place a little before you all descend on it." She saw KK's pout. "At least, declutter and vacuum so we have a cleared space to sit on the floor. It's a small apartment, but it's all mine."

"Yeah, no roommates. I'll never make that mistake again," JJ said, rolling her eyes.

"I'm bringing finger food and a six-pack of whatever strikes my fancy when I'm at the liquor store," KK said. "Anything else, and you'll have to bring yourself."

***

An hour later, Leah opened her door to her coworkers, her first ever real party in North Carolina. Music cranked up, couch pillows thrown on the floor, the theme was an indoor campout. The crew settled into their powwow circle and the stories flew, loud and laugh-filled, no supervisors, patients, or outsiders nearby to offend with their ribald remarks.

Knock, knock.

Billy rapped on the door but got no answer. He opened it a crack and looked in.

"Oh, hey, Billy," Leah called out. "Shoot. I'm sorry. I didn't think we'd be this noisy. It's still bedtime for you, isn't it?"

"Nah, I went to bed early so I could get some shopping done before work. Looks like you're having a party."

"Yeah, a little late for a housewarming party, but better late than never."

"We're having our first 'We don't have to go to work tomorrow so let's get plastered' party," KK said, lifting a bottle of beer in salute. "Wanna join us?"

Billy grinned, then looked down at his wrist where his watch would be if he'd put it on. "Nah, I have to go to work a couple." He spied the bowl of chips and array of veggies, a creamy white dip in the middle of the three friends. "Couple hours, that is. No beer for me. I will let you feed me, though."

"Uh, uh, uh," KK said playfully, wagging a finger in admonition. "First you have to promise to play with us."

"Yeah," JJ said. "We're trying to see who's the biggest *Lost* fan. Audie says she is, but I think it's me."

Billy's eyes widened at the unfamiliar name, then remembered the info on the background check he'd done on her the first day she moved in. That was her legal first name; he had the privilege of calling her by the family moniker. "Oh, *Audie* thinks she is, does she," he mocked.

She looked at him and glared. "Yes, William, I do."

He started to argue that she knew he wasn't a William. He was a Billy, even if it was the only name on his motherless and fatherless birth certificate. She knew it, though. She just didn't want him to call her by her work name. "Touché."

Billy picked up the heavy hardbound copy of *Lost* from the end table and held it up like a prize. "How about you spread out a little and let me see if I can stump all of you? I may not be the biggest fan, but I might have found some shadowy spots hidden in the story you may have forgotten about."

KK scooted closer to JJ. "I'm KK and she's JJ," nodding to the blonde beside him. "You can sit right here," he said, looking up at Billy with an enticing smile and a flirty wink.

Billy flinched. Leah had told him about KK. There was no questioning his gender preference. His tailored scrubs and diamond-studded ear, the come hither look in his eyes practically screamed, 'Dominate me.' Billy also knew of KK's hunger for diversity in partners, his inability to connect on an emotional level with another man. Casual was all this man wanted in his life.

"Or here." Leah pulled another pillow from the couch and set it beside her. "This way I can make sure you don't cheat."

Leah noticed KK's frown of disappointment but ignored it. Billy's uneasiness may not be apparent to others, but she sensed it. She'd seen his eyes light up with attraction in the past. It wasn't there tonight. She'd also seen his chilly, ambivalent demeanor when a guy flirted with him and he wasn't interested. That was the vibe toward KK now. Although Billy's words were friendly, he didn't have a calorie of heat toward KK. Best to sit between the two and keep both men as friends.

Billy took one of the paper bowls beside the snack tray and piled it high with tortilla chips and veggies, then put a heaping spoonful of dip into another. "So, while I'm preloading, how do you want to do this. Maybe a little truth or dare bottle spin to see who's next?" he asked, looking at Leah, then JJ.

Cross-legged, KK bounced up and down like an excited kindergartner. "Ooh, ooh! Truth or dare."

JJ saluted the group with her bottle of beer. "How about Billy asks the spinnee a question? If he or she gets it wrong, then it's truth or dare."

She took a long glug-glub of her beer. Tipping her head all the way back to suck down the last drop, she held it away from her mouth, showboating that it was empty. Chin tucked in, she emitted a mild belch then grinned with pride. "And the bottle is ready!"

Leah took the snacks off the impromptu tablecloth of folded beach towel and set them on the counter. "Oh, here. This will work." She quickly swiped the cutting board with a sponge and held it up.

"Perfect," Billy said, patting the empty space in front of him, ignoring KK's entreating pout. "Set it right here."

"Hey, this isn't fair," KK said. "We don't get to ask Billy any questions."

"I'll tell you what," Billy said, placing the bottle on the board and giving it a trial spin. "I'll let the winner ask me one question. Deal?"

"Ooh, it's gonna be a doozy," KK said.

"Huh?" JJ protested. "You sound pretty sure of yourself. What makes you think you'll win?"

"Hey, hey, now." Leah put up her hands as if trying to calm rough waters. "Let's get started. As they say, the proof is in the pudding. Spin it, Billy!"

The bottle's neck pointed to Leah. "Okay," Billy said, keeping one finger in place in the book while he searched for a harder question. "Aha, what was the name of the scullery maid who brought Sarah the garlic and comfrey for the poultice she first used on Jody?"

Leah thought for a few seconds, then crowed, "Trick question! The first poultice she used was in the field and was made of chewed watercress, not garlic and comfrey. That's one for me. Spin it again."

Billy gave an exaggerated sigh and scowl of defeat. "Oh, all right."

This time, it pointed to KK. Billy ignored the man's excited bouncing and asked, "What was the name of the scullery maid who brought Sarah the garlic and comfrey she used for the first poultice she made *at the castle*?"

"Oh… It was just on the tip of my tongue," KK said, flicking its pink end in and out suggestively as he batted his eyes at Billy.

"Knock it off, KK," JJ said. "You have to be making Billy uncomfortable because I know you're turning my stomach…and I don't have to look at you full on. Just answer the damned question."

"Damned question?" KK argued. "Do not use that word when we're speaking of the most perfect piece of literature ever written by a woman…or a man."

Billy cleared his throat. "Time's up. You have to answer a question or take a dare."

"Time's up? No one said anything about time."

"Standard truth or dare rules," Leah said. "Thirty seconds."

KK pouted and said, "Oh, okay. Truth, I suppose."

"Since it's my place, I get to ask the first question. What does KK stand for? I can't find anything, and human resources said it's none of my business."

"You asked them, too?" JJ chuckled. "I guess I'm not surprised." She saw the teasing, narrow-eyed glare from Leah. "Not that you're a snoop, but that you don't want any mystery unsolved. Oh, that's a compliment, by the way."

"My little detective sister," Billy said and gave her a quick kiss on the cheek.

"Well, reveal time," JJ said. "Tell us."

"My name is Kennedy Kennedy. My mother had a twisted sense of humor. 'If I give you the same first name as your last, it won't matter which one is used: you'll come when called.' My granny was one step ahead of her, though. She started calling me KK from the day she heard what her daughter-in-law had done. It's been KK ever since. So, next spin, Billy."

The bottle landed on JJ. "What was the amount of fabric needed to make a tartan?"

"Trick question!" JJ said with a grin on her face. "It depends on the size of the person and if it's for daily wear of a grand kilt."

"Give me a number for one or any of them," Billy said.

"In the books, Lisa said it's nine yards. However, that's the narrow stuff, about two feet wide. Nowadays, the wider weave is twice that, so only half that amount is needed. I made one and it only took four yards. But I'm not a big person. A big man…"

"Okay, okay," Billy said, hand up. "Nine yards is in the book." He spun again.

"JJ, you get two in a row." He closed the book and opened it to a random page, scanning for inspiration. "Ah, how did Barden Hall get its name?"

JJ immediately answered, "They never said in the stories."

"Oh, yes they did," Billy, KK, and Leah exclaimed, each one talking on top of the other.

Billy held up the book and shushed the trio. "It says here that it was named Garden Hall after the rose garden that was famous for generations. The British were angry the Scots had such beautiful flowers. Every spring, they rode in to wipe out the beds. The roses were hardy and returned despite the abuse. One cruel captain spread salt on the grounds and made the whole yard barren. 'Barren Garden Hall' was shortened to Barden Hall as a cruel joke. The name stuck."

"Where'd you read that?" JJ asked.

"It's a footnote in the back," Billy said, showing her the fine print in the back with the acknowledgments.

"Not fair, not fair," she protested. "I've only read the paperbacks and it's not in those."

"Sorry, honey. It's part of the *Lost* lore written by Lisa Sinclaire, so it still applies," Leah said. "Truth or dare. Oh, and since KK lost the last round, he gets to ask the question."

"Truth or dare," KK asked, a devilish gleam in his eye.

"I don't trust your dares," JJ said. "Truth."

"So, what does JJ stand for?"

"Julissa Julissa Johnson. I guess our mothers were related. They both had the same sick sense of humor. Well, sort of."

KK held out his dark arm next to her pale skin. "I don't think so, sweetie, but you never know. Spin it again, Billy. We have to get a winner so you can get your question asked."

Billy picked up the bottle and held it upright in his lap. He saw KK look at it and smile. He set it to the side and ignored the suggestive wink. "So, you are undeniably three of the biggest fans of *Lost*. As a newbie to the fandom, tell me, what would you change about the stories?"

"Nothing!" they all said, then looked at each other and chuckled at their identical reply.

"Great minds think alike, right?" JJ asked.

"Okay, how about this." Billy shifted in place and leaned forward. "Who in the stories would you most like to meet?"

KK raised his hand like a school child. "Ooh, ooh! I'd like to meet Julian. I think it's so unfair he never got a lover. Well, there was Georgio, but he was a cad and just used Julian for his body. Not that that's a bad thing…"

"Not me," JJ said. "I'd like to meet Sarah and ask her questions about healing. I mean, how could she remember so much stuff? They don't mention it in the books, but surely she had to have a reference journal somewhere. Notes are fine, but good grief! How does she expect to pass down that knowledge? Just give her replacement a fistful of paper and say, 'Figure it out?'"

Billy looked at Leah, "And you, sweetie?"

"To heck with meeting one of them. I'd like to be there myself. You know, be part of the family. Work with them, help build a new America, the whole works. It would be hard, but can you imagine being a part of history?"

Billy jumped at an unfamiliar presence on his knee. KK was scooting back now, bringing his hand to his side.

"What about you, Billy? Who would you like to meet most?" he asked with demure.

"Don't know. I haven't got that far into the series. I've only read the first one. I'm sure there are more interesting characters in the later books. Not that the first crew isn't fascinating. It's just…"

Billy leaned back, looked up at the clock on the microwave, and straightened up again. "Hey, I gotta jet. I still have errands to run before work."

He gave Leah a quick, hard kiss on the mouth, letting her know not to protest his decision. "Love ya, lass. I'll check in with you after work. If you're up to it, I'll make us breakfast. Don't stay up too late. Or do, but don't drink too much. Eggs and hangovers don't go together."

"But you didn't answer my question," KK whined.

132

"I answered 'a' question," Billy said. "Enjoy your party, folks. Go ahead and make as much noise as you want. Nobody will be home next door."

Leah started to get up to see him to the door but saw his minimal headshake. He was out of there!

As soon as the door was closed, KK asked, "I thought he was gay."

Leah shrugged. "He is."

"But he didn't seem interested."

"KK, just because he wasn't interested in you," JJ said, "doesn't mean he's not gay."

"But he kissed you goodbye. And not a little peck on the cheek, either."

"Ach, it's a brother-sister thing," Leah said. "We didn't have siblings so adopted each other."

"Well, I had lots of brothers and sisters and we didn't kiss like that," KK said indignantly.

"As I said, we didn't have them, so no example. We're doing it our own way. We're comfortable and," she leaned forward and got in KK's face, "it's none of your business who or how we kiss, *capiche?*"

JJ smacked him on the shoulder. "I'm with you. I'd like to be kissed by him, too, gay or not. He's a hottie."

"Hands off my brother," Leah said. "Now, TV series marathon or more truth or dare?"

"Put on the wedding episode," JJ said. "We can see who flubs up on reciting the lines first. Mess up and you have to take a drink. And no fair putting it on closed captions."

Chapter 12: Sick of Being Sick

January 2012
Fairbanks, Alaska

"Oh, God. I think I'm gonna die."

Dani rolled over on the couch and gasped at the stabbing back pain, her sudden intake of breath causing the cough to begin anew. Tears streamed down her face and her nose started running again. "Just take me now, please!"

Knock, knock.

She heard the pensive rap on the door but didn't have the breath to call out or the energy to walk over to answer it.

Knock, knock. Harder, more direct this time.

'Either go away or come in. It's not locked,' she thought.

Click.

She heard the door open but didn't have the strength to sit up and see who it was. Her heart raced even faster. Her breathing was shallow – barely a pant – not for fear of being heard, but so she wouldn't start coughing again.

Whoever had come in set something on the counter and stopped. 'Either kill me or leave me alone. No, wait.' Thoughts of the paperwork and the legal mess she'd be leaving behind for Leah smothered her thoughts of dying. 'You have to stay alive at least long enough to get your taxes done. Oh, crap. There are so many loose ends...'

"Eek!"

Startled by a touch, Dani squealed like a startled dog, the fear-induced power-punch of adrenaline sitting her upright for the first time in days. She began coughing again, even harder than before, her breastbone and ribs hurting like they'd been cut in a dozen pieces. She fell back on the couch, the spurt of energy gone as quickly as it had appeared.

"So, are you alive?" Arlie asked.

She nodded but didn't try to speak.

"The newspapers were piling up, so I thought I'd better check on you. You can't talk right? Nod for yes…"

She nodded and sniffed, deliriously happy to have someone with her.

"I'm going to give you a choice. Look at me for a minute, okay?" Arlie squatted down in front of her, checking her pulse and searching her eyes for signs of confusion or clarity.

She looked up and started to cough again.

"Okay, relax and close your eyes. I'll try and make these all yes or no questions. I know you're self-employed."

She nodded.

"And do you have insurance?"

She shook her head.

"That means you have two options, either I call for an ambulance…"

She shook her head adamantly.

"Or I take you to the hospital."

No reply.

"I'm not giving you the option of going to the urgent care clinic instead. You're beyond that. I'm glad you're on a ground-level apartment, though."

She scowled.

"No, not your size. It takes more energy to walk downstairs. My car's already warmed up. Do you mind if I look around for more clothes for you?"

She shrugged and sniffled, wiping her nose on the sleeve of the nightgown she'd worn all week. All the tissues were used up.

"Just a sec." Arlie came back from the bathroom with a roll of toilet paper. "If this is the last roll, I'll get you more. You're in no shape to go shopping. Why didn't you call me?"

"Yes or no," she whispered.

"Huh?"

"You said yes or no questions," she rasped, holding back another round of coughing.

"Yeah. Sorry."

She pointed to the laundry basket on the floor in front of the television.

He brought it to her. She picked through it and found a zip-up hoodie, sweatpants, and a pair of socks.

"Let me help you. We'll just put everything on over your nightgown."

He helped her get dressed, wiped her face with a fresh washcloth, then dabbed her eyes a second time as she started crying again.

"Let's see. I think we have everything." He turned off all but one light and grabbed the keys. He looked around the room and saw her wallet. "They'll want an ID. Is it in here?"

She nodded.

"Come on, darlin'. You're going to get fixed up. I don't know how long you've been sick, but there were three papers out front since I got back from Anchorage. This isn't right. We're going to have to set up a check-in schedule for you. And stop crying, would ya? You're making me weepy. Besides, crying makes you cough."

Dani started to laugh at his antics but knew they brought on more breathing problems. She swished a smile and winked instead.

"Yeah, you're special to more people than you think," Arlie said. "Trust me."

***

"Are you her son," the admitting nurse asked.

"Nope. Good friend and neighbor," Arlie said.

136

"You'll have to wait in the other room then."

"Nope."

"Excuse me?"

He shook his head. "I'm staying here with her. She doesn't have anyone."

"Sir, if you don't leave, I'll have to call the police."

Arlie brought out his badge. "Fast enough for you?"

The nurse gasped, then quickly turned away.

He called out after her, "And send that doctor in here stat."

A chuckle mixed with coughing spasms brought Arlie's attitude back from frustration to concern. "You do know I'm a detective, right?"

Dani nodded, worried that she'd done something wrong when her fever was high, and she couldn't remember it.

"So, my job is to investigate and ask questions."

She nodded again, her expression now blank.

"Here I have someone living just a few yards from me, someone I care about, and I didn't even notice the newspapers stacking up for three days? How dumb am I?"

Dani grinned, fighting back the cough that was rising with the stifled laugh.

"Yeah, well, you think it's funny, but I don't. So much for being top in my class, eh?"

She shrugged then opened and shut her mouth, trying to get him to get closer.

"What? You want to tell me something?" he asked, bending over.

"I'm not dead yet. Good save," she whispered.

He chuckled and kissed her on the forehead, then jumped back. "Geez, woman, you're as hot as a blazing cast iron stove. Damned nurse."

Arlie started pulling out drawers, then saw the cart outside the door loaded with fresh linen. He grabbed a double handful of towels and washcloths and put them in the sink, running cold water over them. "How did I miss that? Damn!"

He squeezed out the small cloth and set it on her forehead, then wrung out the towel. "Here, let me take off that coat. You just lie there and let me do the work."

Arlie's first aid training took over as he put cool cloths over all the bare skin he could find, or in the case of her belly, clear clothes from.

"What are you doing, sir?" the nurse asked, reaching for the toweling.

He turned his back on her, preventing her access to his patient. "I'm doing your job," he said curtly. He shook the towel out to cool it, then put it back. "She's here because she's sick and you didn't even check her for a fever? Who are you?" He snapped a picture of her name tag with his phone, then glared at her. "And where's that doctor?"

"I'm right here. Does there seem to be a problem?"

"She's burning up with fever, can't breathe, and this ignoramus didn't even check her vitals when we came in."

The doctor looked at the nurse, raised an eyebrow, and said, "Get me a thermometer." He pulled his stethoscope off his neck and listened to his patient's heart and lungs. When Dani started another coughing fit, he stepped back, giving her room.

"How long has this been going on?"

"Answer him with fingers," Arlie said. "Don't try to talk."

"Your son?" he asked.

"Coulda been," Arlie said. "Does it make a difference?"

"No, I guess not."

The nurse moved into the doctor's line of sight, wordless, the thermometer in her hand.

"Thank you," he said. "I have this. You can leave."

As soon as she was out of the room, he said, "We're shorthanded. She knows better, and I'd love to send her home, but I don't know if that would smarten her up or not."

"Bring in the Boy Scouts," Arlie said.

"Excuse me?"

"I'm sorry. That was uncalled for. It's just I'm mad at myself, too, for not picking up that something was wrong. She's going to be okay, right?"

"We'll get some fluids in her – she's dehydrated, too – get that fever down, and pump her full of antibiotics. This looks like pneumonia. Maybe have her stay overnight for observation."

Dani started to protest, and a coughing spasm took its place. The doctor turned her on her side so she could breathe easier then looked at Arlie, asking wordlessly what was wrong.

"No insurance," Arlie said, looking at her for verification.

She nodded.

"How about you do what you can do here, throw some prescription samples in there if you have any, and tell me what to look out for? I'll spend the night with her and make sure she stays on track. Will that work?"

"You seem to have a pretty good grasp of what's important, fast reflexes, too. Yes, that'll work. Oh, and she won't be getting a bill from me. I'll see what I can do on the ER visit, too."

***

Two days later

"Are you sure you're okay?" Arlie asked.

"Yes, and if I never see a thermometer again, it'll be too soon," Dani said. "You need to get back to work."

Arlie held up his phone. "I never stopped."

"That's the weirdest looking cell phone I've ever seen," Dani said.

139

"They call them smartphones for a reason. This one's my own design. I made some modifications to it. About the only thing it can't do is print."

"If you can see it on the screen, who cares, right?"

"Exactly. You keep kicking back. I'll be back late this afternoon. I'm bringing home dinner."

"Home?"

"Well, I'll drop by here after I pick up some hot and sour soup for both of us, a few egg rolls for me, and maybe some wontons. I like the company."

"Arlie, your guilt is making me feel guilty," Dani said. "I'll let you take care of me one more day, and then I have to start doing for myself."

"We'll see. Don't forget, helping you makes me feel better, too."

Dani started to cough and quickly grabbed her water bottle, sipping it to pace her breathing. She watched as Arlie studied her, making sure she'd be okay. "Don't worry about me. I have a good book, a fully functional heater, and three different kinds of canned chicken soup. Go out and catch some bad guys, will you?"

"You got it, lady. See you for dinner."

Waiting until she was sure he was gone, Dani picked up the remote and turned on the classic movie channel. "War movie. Ugh." She scanned through all the cable channels she subscribed to, then turned off the TV. "Can't say I didn't look."

She put the remote back on the end table, on top of the book Leah had given her. "Might as well give it another go."

"Damn. Lost my bookmark." She scanned through the first twenty pages, skipping over the twentieth-century parts where Sarah was pissed at her genealogy-obsessed husband who had left her at home while he went on another 'fact-finding' tour, this time to the Rare Arts and Antiquities Emporium in London.

"Let's start here," she said, placing her prescription receipt at page forty. She read a few more paragraphs. "Boring. Who cares who inherited what or who started the trend of putting buttons on jacket sleeves?"

Another few pages skimmed and she saw something she'd missed before. Leah had dog-eared quite a few pages, then smoothed them out. Dani held the book closer to the light found the first page that had been turned under...

Sarah awoke dizzy and disoriented, as if floating on an air mattress on rough seas. Opening her eyes made it worse. Her tummy was in turmoil. Could it be morning sickness? Not a chance, not after what the doctor told her yesterday. She patted the ground beside her making sure she truly wasn't on water.

When she brought up her hand, it was covered in leafy muck. "Ick." She rolled onto her side and she saw she was on a forest floor. How did she get here?

"Alright, Miss Smarty-pants Nurse. What's the last thing you remember?" she said aloud, hoping the use of her authoritative voice would neutralize her fear.

Then it hit her. The news she was barren was the reason she'd taken a taxi to an unknown bar and got plastered. Her husband was probably worried sick.

"Pbht! Worried sick I wasn't going to give him a son. An honest-to-goodness biological half-clone of his own genetics. What? Am I just a vessel? A place to plant his seed so two hundred years from now, some descendent will look him up?"

"Madame, are you lost?" a man asked. "Mademoiselle? Frauline?"

Sarah looked up and saw a redcoat soldier on horseback, a musket laid across his lap at the ready.

"Lost? Oh, I'm more than lost. I'm angry and hungry and frustrated and..."

The soldier suddenly brought up his musket and pointed it into the woods. "Who goes there?"

"What the..." Sarah didn't wait to ask the rest of the question but scrambled to her feet and ran in the direction opposite of where he had the gun pointed.

"Halt!" he yelled after her. "I say, halt or I'll shoot!"

She crouched behind a tree and after a moment of silence, dared a peek in his direction, looking for options.

Bang!

The soldier slumped to the ground. He hadn't been felled by a bullet, though. He been struck in the head by a rock, his finger involuntarily squeezing the trigger and firing harmlessly into the tree in front of him. Blood dribbled from his temple as fist-sized rock splattered in red tumbled down his coat to the ground beside him.

A man wearing a tartan, filthy jacket, and a victor's grim scowl looked away from the fallen soldier to Sarah, his fist still clenched.

She gasped, frozen in place, terrorized by the strangeness of her environment and the sudden violence.

"Come," the young redhaired man said to her, his hand now out to her, beckoning. "Come with me if you want to live."

She flinched and cowered at the sound of a ruckus coming toward them. More soldiers and horses. She nodded and got to her feet, stumbling briefly before chasing after the grungy rock tosser.

The broad-shouldered man broke trail through the thick brush, giving her relatively scratch-free passage to wherever it was he was leading her to. After a few moments, they came to a wide stream, too deep to wade through, too cold to swim across. He ushered her to a cleft at the base of a gnarled willow. The once mighty tree was now hanging precariously from the riverbank, its fallen branches and upended roots providing shelter, a botanical ogre's home that not even a squirrel inhabited. The moist and eerie

142

surroundings were uninviting, but a welcome refuge. The stranger didn't have to tell her to be still. She knew.

The redcoats were still in pursuit, slashing their own path through the bracken, calling out to each other in low tones, telling some to circle about. Their private conversations fluttered about like fluffy down from autumn weeds. They would share the bounty on the big redhaired man. As for the unknown lass, they'd sort that after finding out why she was running about alone and half naked. If she was a lady of worth who had been beset by highwaymen, there'd be a reward, one soldier speculated. Another replied, 'But if not, we'll have sport tonight.'

"Well, this is certainly better than an emotionally controlling husband who's fixated on establishing his bloodline. Poor woman." Dani tore open a new box of tissues and blew her nose, tossing the used wipe into the empty one. "Oh, God, please let me get better."

Rumble, rumble.

Dani looked up at the clock on the wall to verify the time. It couldn't be lunch already, could it? "How'd it get so late? It's almost suppertime."

Knock, knock.

Arlie opened the door and stuck his head in. "Are you decent?"

"Yeah, come on in. I'll be right with you."

After a quick potty break and face washing, Dani was out, all smiles at the company. "What did you bring me? I'm famished."

"I hope you aren't sick of chicken. I saw their chicken chow mein and couldn't help myself. I got enough for both of us."

"Paper plates good enough or do we need something sturdier?"

"We both get our own soup containers, and noodles and wontons are fine on paper plates." Arlie looked in the sink and saw the same two coffee cups that had been there when he left, no dirty pan on the stove. "You didn't eat lunch, did you?"

"Huh?" She brought the paper plates and a couple of forks and spoons to the table.

"No new dirty dishes." He set the Styrofoam cups of soup out and grabbed a few paper towels.

"Do you ever turn off the detective side of your brain?"

"Nope. Born this way. I figured I might as well make money from it." He took out his smartphone, looked at the new message, then held it up to her. "I'd like to make a million on these, but the market isn't here yet. In the meantime, I'll keep the design to myself and continue creating apps that make my job easier."

"Pbbt. If you can make a smartphone that doesn't cost five hundred bucks or more, let me know. Leah and I both need new ones. I wish I could buy one for both of us. She could probably afford a new one, but I can't." Dani nodded to the device on the counter, clear but wrinkled packing tape securing the cracked screen to keep it from falling apart.

"What? Did you forget to ask Santa for one last month?" he joked. "Now, sit down and eat. I'm watching you."

"Yes, Santa. I promise to be a good girl if you bring me a new phone." Dani paused, waiting for another of his snappy retorts.

"Good soup." He bent over the container to slurp another mouthful and wiped a dribble from his chin with the paper towel. He looked up and grinned. "What?"

"You need to get a wife. Or at least a girlfriend. You shouldn't be spending your time with a woman at least twice your age. And fat and infirm at that."

"Ah, but you're youthful on the inside, still sharp and witty, all around good company. Friends don't have to be partner material."

"Yeah, but…"

144

"Hey, *Mom*," he said, pausing for emphasis. "I'll be fine. The right woman will find me when the time is right."

She stared at him as he quickly bowed his head after his declaration. "You're not fooling me, Arlie Biggar. You've already found the right one. You're just too chicken to reach out to her. Or something like that. Either way, you know who you want to be Mrs. Biggar."

Arlie wiped his chin again as his unexpected wide grin caused soup to spill out. "Yeah, well, I may be employed as a detective, but you're pretty sharp yourself. Now, no more talking about this or you might hex me. I'm a man of facts, but I'm also superstitious."

"Works for me," Dani said. She picked up her spoon and realized she was looking in the living room, eager to get back to *Lost*. Suddenly, she didn't want the book to end. She wanted more!

Chapter 13: Solar-powered

February 14, 2012

"What's this?" Dani asked, inspecting the box meticulously wrapped in repurposed brown paper bag.

"A gift," Arlie said, avoiding her inquiring stare.

"I love you, mister, but I am not your Valentine."

"Oh, shoot! I didn't even realize that was today. No, no. Don't take offense. It's just a gift. It was time. I mean, sometimes it's right. I mean, the gift is right. I didn't realize the time was wrong. I mean, I didn't think about it at Christmas, and didn't know…"

"Stop babbling. I think I know what you mean. Forced occasions for gift giving sucks." She held up the box and shook it gently. "You saw this and thought of me, right?" He nodded. "Oh, that's so sweet."

She used a table knife to slip between the evenly spaced snips of tape, then tore it off the rest of the way. "Aw, two stacked white boxes. Homemade building blocks? Nah. No brand names or logos on the packaging, either." She sniffed it. "Not chocolates, dang it."

"This wasn't supposed to take all day," Arlie said. "But I do want to know what you think of it…or them. There's two and they're pretty much the same; one for you and one for Leah."

"Now you've got my curiosity piqued. It can't be clothes because we don't wear the same size. Plus, the boxes are too small. Hair adornments, maybe?"

"If you don't hurry up, I'll open it myself."

"Okay, okay. I'm just messing with you." Dani picked up the knife again and slit the cellophane tape holding the two boxes together. "Which one's mine?"

"Would you just open the box? I put your initials on yours, otherwise they're identical."

146

"How'd you know my middle name. No, wait. Not only did you see my drivers' license, you probably know more about me than I do."

Arlie shrugged and grinned. "One of my talents."

"Talents or skills, valuable whether inherited or learned," she babbled as she tried to take the lid off one of the boxes without tearing it apart. "I guess it doesn't matter how it came to you, but how you use it…"

Her words stopped. She ran her finger across the flawless glass then looked up at him.

"Do you like it?"

"Duh? Of course, I do. Is this what I think it is, Arlie? A phone?"

"Yup." He pried it out of the box with the tip of one finger and turned it on its side. "Ah, this is yours. See? DUM."

She chuckled. "I would have changed back to my maiden name after I divorced, but DUD was just as bad."

"Danielle Ursula Madigan." Arlie shrugged. "Ursula. She-bear. Yeah, I'll bet you could be a real tough she-bear if someone crossed you."

"Oh, Leah is going to be giddy with glee. We've been emailing back and forth because her phone won't work unless it's on speaker. She doesn't want the world to hear her calls, so ignores everything but texts. And I hate texting!"

"Well, you can text, email, or call on this. You can video chat on it, too."

"Don't you have to have a special program or app or whatever they call it, for that?"

"Yup, but mine's built in. These two are betas of my own design. Oh, and no excuse for not knowing where your changer is. There's a universal port on this one, plus…" Arlie turned it over to show her the dark matte gray reverse side. "It has a solar charger built in. As long as it's not nighttime or too cloudy, you can charge the phone in the sun. Just don't leave it in a car on a hot day. Just like any other electronics, it'll toast it."

She took it back from him, then picked up her reading glasses. "Who's Almost Alchemy? Is that your company?"

"Shoot. I forgot to pull that off. That's just a prototype logo." He pulled off the tiny white picture of two A's floating out of a cauldron. "I kind of liked the name. It fits with what I'm doing. Great idea, lousy timing, though. There's little interest in solar-powered devices these days with the cheap cost of electricity. No one wants to bother using all that free fuel just pouring off the sun. I'll probably hold back on releasing the idea for a few years."

Arlie huffed in frustration, then noticed the time on the microwave. "Hey, I have a work thing I have to do. Check out the phone. Play around with it. You can't break it. At least, not accidentally. It isn't bulletproof or hammer-proof but is waterproof and built to withstand being dropped from ten feet. Once powered up, the old data will automatically transfer to the new one. Another little perk to this design."

Arlie clicked the power button and the screen popped to life immediately. "You're set. I don't think you'll master all the apps before I get back, but probably enough of them to keep you busy for a day or two. Great camera, too. Works for stills or video."

"My own private movie studio. Cool. Everything but print, you say?"

"Just about. I really do have to go. Enjoy!"

"Hey, wait."

Arlie took his hand off the doorknob. "What?"

Dani gave him a big hug and squeeze. "Happy Valentine's Day. Remember what you told me when I was so sick? You're special to more people than you think? Well, back at ya."

"Happy Valentine's Day to you, too."

***

148

"You got a package," Billy said. "The letter carrier said it wouldn't fit in the box and someone forgot to put the parcel box key back."

"So, she gave it to you?"

Billy wiggled the small box a foot from her face, then pointed to her name on it. "Duh. Oh, and since she was already here, I gave her back the parcel box key, too. It was me…"

"It's from my mom," Leah said, grabbing it from him before he decided to play keep away. "I wonder what it is. Too late for Christmas and not my birthday yet."

"You're so lucky," Billy said. He held up the nearly empty carafe. "Do you want more coffee?"

"Not that old stuff. If you make another pot, I'll have some. So, what do you mean I'm so lucky?"

Without being asked, Billy handed her the pair of scissors from the drawer. "You have a mom. Plus, she sends you gifts for no reason at all. Why don't you ever talk about her?"

Leah sliced through the tape on the box and pulled another box out of it. Silent. Frowning.

"You didn't answer my question," Billy said, dumping out the old coffee.

"What question?"

He turned on the faucet, gave the glass urn a quick rinse, then filled it with water. "Why don't you ever talk about her?"

Leah shrugged. "What's there to talk about?"

"Geez, Leah," Billy said, frustrated. "I don't know. I never had a mother. Are you two alike? Do you look like her? Do you have any of the same traits? Is she in the health care industry, too? Where does she live? Scratch that. I see the package was shipped from Fairbanks, Alaska. Did you ever spend any time there? Did you watch the northern lights together? Is she coming here for a visit any time soon? Will I get a chance to meet her?" He huffed

149

in exasperation, then grabbed the scoop out of the coffee can too roughly, scattering grounds all over the counter and sink.

Leah looked at him and blinked, shocked. "Are you okay? You seem a little testy."

"Testy? Yeah, I'm testy. Frustrated in about six different ways, four of them I can't talk about – or shouldn't. But really, I don't know what's going on between you two, and why she's such a secret, but believe me, having a mother is a blessing. Unless she did something horrible, I would think you'd call her at least once a week. Does she even know I'm alive? That I'm your best friend and if something went wrong, I'd be the person to contact?"

Billy calmed down slightly at his last remark. "Leah, I don't have anyone. I mean, I know you'd be there for me if something happened like I got sick or hurt, but there's no one for you to tell. If I died, that's it. A corpse for you to take to the crematorium, then scatter the ashes wherever your heart desires. I have no homeland. I live in an apartment. Working is my life."

Leah set the scissors down, leaving the inner box a mystery for another moment. "My parents split after I got out of high school. I was ticked. Then my dad got cancer. Mom probably wouldn't have gone through with the divorce if she'd known about it, but he didn't tell her for that reason."

"From what you just said, it sounds like he was okay with it. Was there some big event – and if so, I don't want or need to know what it was – that caused the split?"

"Huh?"

Billy whispered, "Like drugs, infidelity, a change in sexual orientation…"

"No, and certainly no infidelity. They just weren't happy."

"And so by splitting up, they thought they'd be happier. Were they?"

"Maybe. I don't know." Leah paused, rubbing her index finger along the edges of the little white box, thinking about what Billy

150

had said. "I don't know if they were happier, but I think they were both less miserable. Does that make sense?"

"Sounds like something from my high school psychology class. Parents staying together for the kids. As soon as they're gone, empty nest syndrome occurs. Nothing for them to focus on as a couple. They drift apart unless they can find something in common. Golf or tennis maybe."

"Less miserable on their own terms." Leah chuckled. "I've been trying to figure it out for almost five years now. Suddenly, it makes sense."

"Glad I could help," Billy pressed the button on the coffee maker and snatched the box out of Leah's hand. "Now, let's sit on the couch and see what treasures Mom sent us."

"Billy!" Leah screeched, chasing him around the small room, reaching for the box in a juvenile game of keep away. "Mom, he's pickin' on me."

Another minute or two of horseplay, then Billy ended it by plopping down on the love seat, box held close to his chest. "Will you share it with me?"

Leah held her hand out. "If it's edible, yes. Otherwise, Mom sent it to me…so there!" and stuck out her tongue.

Billy burst out laughing. "God, I missed so much. Thanks. I think I'm out of my testy funk."

"Well, I missed it, too. Let's see what Mom got us." Leah stuck her thumbnail under the tape holding the box together, then pried it apart.

"Oh, my God! It's a phone. A gorgeous smartphone. Look at the size of that screen."

Billy looked over her shoulder. "I've never seen one that fancy. It looks like a computer that when through a Willy Wonka miniaturizing machine."

Leah picked it up and turned it over, setting the box aside.

Billy picked up the box and looked in the lid. "Here's a note. It says, 'From my friend Arlie for you. I have its twin. All set up. Give me a call when you feel up to it. Love, Mom.'" He handed her the note. "Pretty cool friend. I'd like to meet Arlie or any other guy or gal who just gives out smartphones…in pairs!"

"Here," Leah handed him the phone and stood up. "You check it out. I don't feel too swift. I'm going to bed. Maybe a two-hour nap will do me more good than a cup of coffee. Why are days off so hard to adjust to?"

Billy set the phone aside and followed her to the door. "I'm not so sure it's the day but the fact you just had a major life revelation. Let it settle in for a while. Don't try to figure it out. It is what it is. I doubt anything you could have done or said would have changed anything."

"Pbbt! Except maybe being born. I'm the reason they got married in the first place. Try living with that."

"Trade ya."

"Huh?"

"Hey, at least they kept you. I was dropped off at a hospital. Talk about rejected! But for both of us, we didn't do anything wrong. We are what we are. We make choices hundreds of times a day. Being born was never one of them. Go forth and make the world a better place, Leah." Billy kissed her on the cheek. "After you take a nap."

Chapter 14: Lost and Lost Again

July 2012
Fairbanks, Alaska

The chill settled on them like frost on a pair of mushrooms. He settled her near him, pulling his plaid close about her face, leaving a small gap for fresh air. Her ragged breath escaped from the opening, rising like steam from kettle, a thin wispy plume assuring him that even if she was deathly ill, she was still alive.

Sarah was seldom bothered by any sickness. Even the ague passed her by every season. This had to be something else. Could it really be the hex that Old Man MacLeod cast on her for impugning his authority? No one could deny she had the right as a healer to admonish him to remove the perils that affected the children's safety and health. Telling him the young ones needed to subsist on more than apple pulp, and that safety barriers should be placed in front of the press mechanisms was part of her duty. Adding that it wouldn't hurt his orchard and cider press business if he set aside a bit of land as a vegetable garden may or may not have been her Christian responsibility. However, it was definitely not her job to voice aloud her suspicion that all fifteen children working for him couldn't be his own and suggest that at least some were the missing youth from the coast. Once again, her outspoken twentieth-century indignation and sense of right and wrong had put her in peril.

As loud as the man's response was to her accusation – a grandiose and theatrical hex complete with broad gestures and a smoke bomb – it wasn't the source of her malady. Jody knew they were just words meant to impress the bystanders and terrorize the children. Sarah had shrugged off the performance with a long string of crude words said under her breath. Hours later though, *her health was failing. The old man had to have done something to her, but what?*

Then Jody recognized the smell. Her breath smelled acrid, almost like burnt almonds. He pulled back the plaid and sniffed closer. Cyanide. Sarah had told him about it, how minute quantities of it were in the seeds of apples and other fruits. It was possible to make a poison from it...if one had enough seeds.

And Old Man MacLeod ran one of the biggest cider presses in the valley. Folks came from near and far for his services. They'd stop at his cidery on their way into town to get supplies, their wagons filled with bushel baskets of fallen apples. When they returned with their dry goods and other purchases, they would have left room for the kegs of juice to take home and process into hard cider. Old man MacLeod probably had more raw material for cyanide than any three men in the colony put together.

"What did ye tell me about poisoning, Sarah?" Jody asked, trying to rouse her. "Ye have to help me..."

"Whatcha reading there, Arlie?" Marc asked, jolting his joint task force co-worker out of the eighteenth century.

"Oh, it's that time travel romance everyone's talking about. At least, it's the first one in the series. My neighbor gave it to me. She said it might help me find my romantic inner self. Pbbt."

"Dani?"

Arlie nodded, trying to hide his chagrined smile.

"You sure spend a lot of time with her. Isn't she about seventy years old?"

"Sixty," Arlie said. He pointed to his temple. "Still got it up here, though."

"Sharp, single, and sixty," Marc joked. "Two out of three ain't bad, but not right for you. Too bad she isn't about thirty years younger."

Arlie rolled his eyes but remained mute. He'd thought of that a few times himself.

Marc pointed to the couple on the book cover. "Yeah, Dottie's read all of these. She made me read the first one. This is the one I already read. I told her I couldn't get into it with all the colloquialisms and psychological analysis of the crazy people. I'm more of an action guy – guns and conflict, motorcycles and mayhem. She could just fill me in on the storylines in the later books, who fights who and all that stuff. After reading this, I'm pretty well acquainted with the characters – actually, more than I feel comfortable with, if you know what I mean."

"Yeah, I do. I'm more of a 'let's leave the lovin' part behind closed doors' kind of guy. I don't need details. I guess that's the stuff that sells books, though." Arlie put the book down. "Then again, this isn't what I'd consider erotica. It's more fantasy and action adventure than romance if you ask me. At least, so far. Time travel. If only it were real."

"What time would you go back to?" Marc asked, picking up the book and rereading the back cover.

"Oh, I'd just zip back to about four years ago."

"Where's the fun in that?"

"I'd just make a different choice," Arlie said, his eyes staring off in the distance, thinking of Charlene, abandoned by her fiancé, pregnant with his anonymously donated seed. Why hadn't he contrived a way to meet her. And the son he'd fathered. *One of these days, I will.*

"Come on," Marc said, punching him in the shoulder. "Get out of La La Land and back to Alaska. I got a line on the De Luca Brothers. They're in your neighborhood and haven't done anything wrong, but I have my suspicions. Their fly-in hunting trip might be multi-purpose."

"Big game hunting and salmon fishing might be the reasons why they came to Fairbanks, but since the Grand Jury is meeting next month in Anchorage, I'd say they're here for more than that.

Maybe a little diversion before starting the real business end of scouting and hunting down witnesses who've agreed to speak up."

"Yeah," Marc added. "Bag their limit of four-legged game before going after the two-legged kind."

"Keeps us employed. To protect and to serve."

Chapter 15: Looking for Misters Right

July 2012
Greensboro, North Carolina

She would recover! Joy and relief overwhelmed him. Tears sprang from his bleary eyes, red-rimmed with fatigue. He bent over, ready to cover her face with kisses, then grimaced and backed away. They'd both feel better if he performed a more thorough toilet. Jody poured fresh water into the wooden bowl he employed as a basin and rinsed out the homespun rag again. A third time he wiped her face, appreciating the curl of each dark eyelash, the gentle flare of her nostrils, the little divot dimple in her chin. Awestruck and in love all over again, he decided fresh air was more important for her recovery than the removal of miniscule vestiges of her ordeal.

His change of position startled her. "What? What happened?" she stammered, reaching up to touch his face, glad he was substance and not a vision.

"Yer back. I thought I'd lost ye for sure this time. It wasna sickness but poison. I...how do ye call it? I helped ye clear yer stomach."

Sarah swallowed tentatively. "Is that why my throat's sore? You jammed your finger down it to make me puke?"

Jody smiled weakly and shrugged. "Ye did say to get rid of the offensive matter, aye?"

"Aye." Sarah looked at the cup on the small table beside Jody. "Is that water?"

"It is." He held the back of her head and brought the cup near, ready to help her drink, then hesitated. "Unless ye'd rather have tea. I can brew a pot fer ye. I also have whiskey but I dinna think that would be soothing on yer raw waim."

157

Sarah glared at him, her mouth inches from the cup. "Just give me a damned drink of whatever's closest. My mouth tastes like the bottom of a chicken coop."

"Are you reading again?"

Leah's question startled Billy back to reality. "Of course. And it's your own fault that my laundry isn't getting done or dishes washed. You've got me so wrapped up in these books, I can't pull myself away. Shoot, I even considered taking a sick day so I could finish that first book."

"Why didn't you? KK and JJ told me they both took a day off when the last book came out."

"Pbbt. There's not enough extra manpower around here to cover legitimate absences much less mental health days. Do you want to hear about another unsolved case? You're pretty good at figuring these out." Billy put the book down and went to the kitchen.

"If you're thinking of making coffee, don't," Leah said. "Too hot. Plus, I made a gallon of sun tea. This time, I threw in a sprig of fresh mint. So, go ahead and ask. But no fair giving me another one of those cases you already solved. That was just mean."

Billy chuckled. "Hey, I was testing your psychic abilities. You claim it's just great deductive reasoning, but you and I both know you have ESP. Admit it."

"I'll admit I have a very keen sixth sense, but since I've never been tested, there's no proof."

"I can get you set up for an evaluation. I have a friend who has a friend…" Billy paused at her scowl. "But you don't want to be tested and have it verified, right?"

Leah shrugged. "And have it known far and wide that I'm a freak?"

"Gifted," Billy said, coming in for a hug.

158

She leaned into his arms for a brief squeeze, then backed away. "Too hot. Do you have any ice? I'm out. The tea's cold, but it would be better chilled."

"Yeah, a nice sweaty glass of iced tea poolside, a good book, and intermittent dips to cool down."

"Nope."

"Why not?" Billy asked.

"Because I'm borrowing your air mattress. I want to float and read. Oh, and make sure we use plastic cups. No glass around the pool, remember?"

"What? Are you the pool police?" Billy asked. "And how come you're always borrowing everything. I know you have enough money to afford a five-dollar air mattress."

"Because I don't want to accumulate 'stuff.'" She looked at him and grinned. "Because one of these days, I'm gonna be out of here, and I don't want to leave tons of duplicates for you to get rid of."

"*Me* get rid of? What? Am I your mother?"

"Nope, but you are my significant other. Oh, by the way, I put that in writing. ICE – In Case of Emergency – you're the go-to person."

"Well, if I am – and I don't have a problem with that since I already did that with you – you have to give me the contact info for your mother."

Leah sighed. "It's in my phone. You probably already downloaded all the contacts in there anyhow."

"Hey, you told me I should. I didn't do it without permission."

"But I was drunk…"

"As if that ever made a difference."

"Oh, by the way," Leah said, grabbing the ice tray out of the freezer, "my mom is coming out for a visit. She asked if it's okay if she stayed here."

"You said yes, I hope."

"Duh! I'm not going to tell her no. I did say it was a one bedroom, one bed apartment, but the couch was comfy."

"She could stay at my place and you and I could share your bed," Billy offered, excitement brightening his face.

"No. My bed's smaller than yours. And hey, innocent or not, I don't want her to know we sleep together."

Billy frowned at her but didn't say a word.

"Besides, we work different shifts. She's only coming out for five days. Don't get too wound up, though. She won't be here until just before Halloween. I've never been in Alaska at that time of year, but she says Fairbanks is the pits then. Dark, dreary, and all that crap. Plus, she hears we have awesome autumns."

"The brightest and boldest around," Billy said.

"Just like you," Leah said. "Come on, grab those air mattresses and I'll get the drinks and books. Time to get *Lost*!"

"Ah, *Lost*, the greatest time travel romance of all time. How did I ever live without it?"

***

Three weeks later

"I think my date was worse," Leah said.

"Nope. It was mine. Actually, mine was not only worse, it was *the worst* date of all time," Billy said dramatically, then toned it down and added, "but I'll let you tell me about yours first. Then we'll see."

"Mine was so bad, I was ready to swear off dating forever," Leah said. "Or maybe just check out dating women instead. Nah, I work with them. I wouldn't want to bed one. Too needy."

"I'll bet I could introduce you to one or two who might change your mind."

"Doesn't make a difference whether male or female, I've given up on dating," Leah said and grabbed the bottle of wine. "Full disclosure time, dude. Get ready to weep."

"I don't weep," Billy argued.

Leah looked down her nose at him. "What about when we watched the end of the season cliffhanger for *Lost*? You were a four-tissue mess!"

"Yeah, well that was different. Or not. Hell, you're supposed to be convincing me your date was the worst, not making me feel bad because I have a sensitive nature hidden beneath my detective badge. Cops have feelings, too. We just aren't supposed to show it."

"At least in public," Leah said and blew him an air kiss.

He caught the kiss and patted it onto his cheek. "Popcorn? Or will your story take that long? It's sure taking a long time to get started."

"Cheese puffs." Leah held up the bottle. "You're supposed to have cheese with wine, not corn. And bring napkins, too."

Billy brought a stack of red plastic cups, the bag of cheese curls, and a roll of paper towels. Leah separated the cups while he opened the chips, holding two cups out for him to pour the snacks into. He pulled the cork out of the wine with his teeth while Leah waited with two more cups for him to fill.

"See, this is what we need," Leah said.

"What? Wine? Of course, we need wine after a crappy night."

"No, what we have here. Two bodies, one spirit. You don't have to tell me what to do and vice versa. And don't say you're psychic because you're not."

Billy chuckled. "And by asking that question you once again proved you are. Don't worry, I've given up on trying to get you paid for the little insights you give me. There's already one psychic consultant. Not that we can find her when we need her…"

"And that's because she's psychic and knows you're looking for her. Kind of hard to play reverse hide and seek with a seer, right?"

"Yeah. You're right, though. Leah, I know as sure as we're sitting here – whining in each other's wines and planning to get

161

wasted – that there is someone out there for both of us. I can't, won't, don't believe that we're meant to be alone and without a soul mate. We just have to be patient and wait."

Leah snorted, then downed her drink in one long swallow. "And not go crazy while we wait."

Billy started his story without preface. "Left me with the bill when he went to the john. He didn't know I had gone back to the servers' station for more napkins and saw him hooking up with another guy. A second later, he split with him, tearing out of the restaurant parking lot, cuddled up to the bruiser on the back of the dude's tricked-out Harley."

Leah held her cup out for a refill. "Pretty much the same here except mine took off with a blonde bimbo in a classic Corvette."

Billy finished pouring her drink, set the bottle down, then lifted his red cup in salute. "Tie."

"How much was your bill?" Leah asked, holding off on the toast.

Billy swished his lips, thinking. "Before or after adding in the bar bill I rang up after he left?"

"Tie," Leah said and clunked her cup into his. "Don't ever leave me, Billy. I don't think I could stand it."

"Even if Mister Right comes along, sweetie, I'll never give up on you."

"Ditto. Let's just hope we both meet our Misters Right at the same time. No lag time for loneliness."

"Ditto. Cheers."

Chapter 16: Vacation

October 28, 2012

"Are you sure it's not a problem? I can call a taxi?"

"Dani, you don't want to get in the back of one of those. Drunks puke in them. Or worse. There aren't enough little pine tree air fresheners in the world to cover up that stench."

"Arlie, you're one of a kind. Oh, and when I'm gone, I'd like you to do me a favor."

"Water your plants, feed your dog? Say it, and I'll do it."

"I don't have any plants, and you know I don't even own a goldfish. The thermostat's set to sixty and I put the lights on a timer like you suggested, but I want you to read these." Dani handed him a box of colorful paperback books.

He picked up the one on top. "*Lost*? I already read it. You gave me a copy, remember?"

Dani took it back. "The rest are for you. I was taking this one to reread on the trip. You're a great guy, too good to be spending all your time at work. If you're not going to date, treat yourself to an hour or two of reading every night. Or morning, depending on when your shift ends. Bring out the romantic in you. I know it's in there. And as sure as I'm standing here, I'm certain you'll find Miss Right. I believe in no time at all, you'll have little redheaded Arlie Juniors running around."

Arlie laughed out loud and shook his head. "Mini me's? Oh, wouldn't that be a kick?" He turned away and set the box on the counter by the door. *There's already one running around in Arizona. I just need to figure a way to catch up to him and introduce myself to his mother.*

"I'm serious. You're going to be old before your time. You've told me I'm a young soul in an old body. I thank you for that. It's really flattering and well, I kind of feel the same way. Lots of older people do, though. I think. No, I'm sure. Anyhow, you're just the opposite, at least to a degree. You're an older man in a young body. Get out, take a vacation to a warm state this winter. See what it feels like to go swimming on Christmas Day instead of being ice-bound at minus forty."

Arlie felt his smile grow. "Could be worse. I could be in Prudhoe."

"No cops up there last I heard," she said. "But yes, there are colder places in the world than Fairbanks. Speaking of that, did you ever find out about that opening in Anchorage? At least, it's a little warmer and brighter down there."

"The Banana Belt?" He picked up a book out of the box and looked at the back cover. "Yeah, I got it. I'll be moving out before the end of November. Crappy time to relocate, but since it's just a few boxes of personal items and I'm not interfering with anyone's big Thanksgiving or Christmas get-togethers, it won't be much different than bugging out in June."

"Except when your arms are loaded, it's hard to keep the door shut and lights on when coming in and going out. Hey, I'll be back in less than a week. I'll hold doors and flip light switches for you. Oh, and I have a tape gun and know how to use it."

"Tape gun?"

Dani reached into a cabinet and pulled out the packing tape dispenser. "Tape gun. Never leave home without it."

"Speaking of that." Arlie picked it up and taped the box of books closed. "I promise I'll look at them tonight."

"I should have set you up with them sooner. The first was good, but they really do keep getting better and better. Sometimes I think I'd love to live back then, and other times it scares the dickens out of me."

"Well, Danielle, it doesn't make a difference because you're stuck with me and the billions of other nuts in the twenty-first century."

"Yeah, bummer, huh?"

"Sometimes, I think so," Arlie said. "Sometimes."

***

Four hours later
Anchorage International Airport

"Look at that!" Vinnie hissed. "It's her!"

Hugo turned to look but Vinnie pulled him back sharply. "She'll see you!"

"Who? Who am I hiding from?"

Vinnie grabbed a pair of sunglasses from the airport kiosk display, bit off the price tag, and handed them to Hugo. "Put these on. Remember why we came up here in the first place?"

Hugo chuffed. "Came up? Got stuck here for over a year, you mean."

"Yeah, well that's the 'Dan' person we were supposed to give an attitude adjustment to," Vinnie said pointing with his thumb at Dani, who was seated thirty feet away, reading a book.

"I never saw the woman, and she never saw me, so how would I know if that's her or not?"

"Because I'm tellin' you." Vinnie grabbed another pair of sunglasses and repeated the tag removal, scraping off the little plastic 'UV Protection' label. "Now we look like the Blues Brothers. Go steal that guy's guitar."

"Which guy?"

"The one with long hair who's sleeping with a guitar case at his feet, dumm… dear brother."

Hugo glared at him, knowing that the biggest airport in Alaska was not the place to start a ruckus with his brother or anyone else.

165

Their ID barely slipped past the myopic agent in Barrow. It might not pass security's inspection here.

The two had been stuck in Alaska since they escaped police custody fourteen months earlier. Wanted posters were everywhere. Surrounded by ocean or Canada, they were unable to leave by air, land, or sea without being ID checked by some sort of transportation security. Rather than chance it, Vinnie decided they could get easy jobs and build a history with new names and addresses. During that time, they'd done everything from sweeping floors to inspecting roads and waterways to counting salmon and watching inactive volcanoes. Their stolen and modified credentials bolstered their fake portfolios as environmental experts, even though neither one of them could spell either word.

Hopping from one remote site to another with verbal job referrals from their drinking buddies, they always took their wages in cash because 'their bank accounts had been compromised.'

The fun had run out now. Someone had said Vinnie reminded him of a two-bit thug he'd known in Brooklyn. Although no one believed the man, Vinnie knew it was time to leave. A few nuggets of stolen gold and a wad of honestly earned cash, and they were on their way back to New York.

"I kinda got to like this place," Hugo said. "Except for the mosquitos. Hey, if it doesn't work out back east, how about we come work on The Slope again. Man, those oil rig cooks made the best food ever!"

"Not a chance," Vinnie said. "You got so fat, they don't make insulated coveralls big enough for you. You'd best start looking for a job in the desert. We can always find a tentmaker to fix you up."

Smack! Without thinking, Hugo slapped Vinnie on the back of the head, a reflexive move at being insulted. "Oh, there was a big mosquito," he said, giggling.

Vinnie looked around. He didn't believe him, but once again, his dumb brother had figured a way to get away with causing trouble. It would feel great to pummel him but spending months or years in jail because he'd been arrested for a disturbance – fingerprinted and forced to make up unserved time all the way back to his juvenile detention days – wouldn't.

"Come on, Hugo. Let's go back east and raise some hell."

The End

This is the end of Lost: The Time Travel Romance That Started It All but the beginning of *so* much more.

Everyone's story begins somewhere, and this is the place for a few in the Catenated Universe.

Do you wish Jody and Sarah were real? (Spoiler Alert: They are! Find them throughout *The Fairies Saga* series).

Do you want to know what happens to Dani when she arrives in North Carolina for a visit? Is she that 'Dan' character referred to on the note attached to The Letters? Read *Naked in the Winter Wind*, first book in *The Fairies Saga* series.

How about James and Clotilde? Can James get rid of his gold digger wife? And Billy and Leah, do they ever find their true loves? More about them in *Aye, I am a Fairy*, also part of *The Fairies Saga*.

How about Arlie and Marc? Will Arlie ever find the nerve to meet Charlene and the son he sired as an anonymous sperm donor? Check out the *Arlie Undercover* series, starting with *A Stingray Christmas*.

Will we ever meet the mysterious Marty? Yes! Check out *Dances Naked*, the story of the British lord who is lost in eighteenth-century Cherokee lands. Part of *The Fairies Saga* Series.

What happens to Vinnie and Hugo? Check out *That Twin Thing* for more of their nefarious efforts.

Meet André the 'Real' Giant and follow him on a few exploits in *The Set Up* and *They Call Me Sherlock,* stories in *Triplets: Three Aren't One* series.

Enjoy the Catenated Universe of these four series where Billy the good-natured detective pops in and out, making friends wherever he goes.

About the Author

Author Dani Haviland started writing late in life and has been making up for lost time with a flood of works from sports, gritty tales, time travel, and Sweet and Sassy romances to Unforgettable romantic suspense, Cute But Crazy rom-coms, and cozy mystery stories – with some Short Stories thrown in to round out the reading experience.

Dani is also the owner of Chill Out! Books, one of the publishers for The Authors' Billboard. Follow her on BookBub to make sure you get her latest stories.

Contact information:
Website: **www.danihaviland.com**
Facebook: **https://www.facebook.com/dani.haviland/**
BookBub: **http://bit.ly/BBDani**
Email: **dani@danihaviland.com**
Twitter: @dani_haviland, @gr8authors

I love to hear from readers!
Sign up for my newsletter to get the latest information on new releases, free stuff, and contests here: **http://bit.ly/2DHnews**

Awesome readers group!
I have a Facebook Page for folks who are interested in early excerpts and insights into my latest books and box sets plus the latest from some of the authors and box sets I publish under Chill Out! Books.. I'd appreciate it if you'd like the page. Drop in and see if I've remembered to add photos and excerpts of my works in process.
Dani Haviland & Friends Readers Group:
https://www.facebook.com/ChillOutDani

Other Books by Dani Haviland

ARLIE UNDERCOVER SERIES (romantic suspense based in Alaska and Arizona)

A Stingray Christmas: (Book One) Anchorage detective on medical leave travels from Alaska to Arizona to see for the first time the son he'd fathered as an anonymous sperm donor. Great and rotten surprises await the cop with the smartest smartphone around.

The Biggest Heart Ever: (Book Two) When would Arlie learn that trying to do everything by himself could be deadly—and make Charlene a widow before they were married?

Always a Bigger Fish: (Book Three) Back in Alaska, Arlie finds out he's a target. Will vacationing detective Billy Burke (from THE FAIRIES SAGA) have information to help nab the scalper?

How to Fix a Broken Life: (Book Four) When Arlie's very pregnant wife is kidnapped by pseudo terrorists, will he be the one to rescue her or will a surprise hero come in to save the day?

Because You Said So: (Book Five) Something's amiss at the Port of Anchorage. Will Arlie be able to solve it and still be back in time to wear the Santa suit?

Heaven and Heartbreak (Book Six) Sharing her child with a gay father and his lover was the easy part. Finding a woman for herself seemed impossible.

THAT TWIN THING SERIES (romantic suspense series)

The Midwife's Son: The midwife refused her selfish patient's request to smother the scrawny twin and instead took him home to bring up as her own. Years later, will the two young men wind up in each other's lives despite the midwife's efforts to keep them apart?

Phoenix I'm Not: Will the billionaire's spoiled son be resurrected from the ashes of his former life of drugs and mayhem by love or be tortured and eliminated by the assassin sent by his mother?

170

<u>Lost and Found Family</u>: Separated at birth, these twins find they have more than genetics in common: they're both the target of killers who are willing to risk everything to take them out.

<u>Peter Elph</u>: A supplement to the story of Lost and Found Family, this short story is about a member of the Wagner family back in 1886 Tombstone, Arizona.

<u>That Twin Thing: The Complete Collection</u>: All four books in one place.

THE FAIRIES SAGA SERIES (historical fiction/time travel, listed in order with novellas):

<u>Kibbles and Bits</u>: FREE ebook: Sample the first stories in the series before you buy. The Fairies Saga stories. Find out how the first five books got their crazy names, too.

<u>Naked in the Winter Wind</u>: (Book One) How does an older woman wind up as a young hottie in Revolutionary War era North Carolina?.

<u>Ha'Penny Jenny</u>: (Book Two) More about the naïve and psychic young girl who was adopted into a time traveling family. Will her past catch up to her?

<u>Aye, I am a Fairy</u>: (Book Three) Young British lord finds himself entwined with a time traveling family and must decide if he should go back in time, too.

<u>Dances Naked</u>: (Book Four) Directionally challenged time traveler is rescued by Cherokee in 18th century. What must he do before the chief will show him to The Trees, the portal through time?

<u>Chasing Christmas</u>: (Book Five) A young Cherokee is rescued from an abusive man and changes the lives of many in this 18th century America family.

<u>The Great Big Fairy</u>: (Book Six) Very tall Benji grew up in the 20th century but was born in the 18th. When he finds a way to

return to his grandparents in the distant past, he goes for it. Once there, he realizes he can't stay, but must return to the future.

Little Bear and the Ladies: (Book Seven) What's a bachelor trapper to do with all the females he rescues from the Hessian mercenaries? He'd better hurry and figure something!

Little Drummer Boy: (Book Eight) Young Scout works to earn money for a home in post-Revolutionary War America but runs up against prejudices and snowstorms.

Never Too Young: (Book Nine) Scout and Ha'Penny Jenny have grown up, but will they be able to spend their life together, or will the past and ruffians get in their way?

Time in a Little Blue Bottle: (Book Ten) Elvis, Mark Twain, and the prime vampire are racing to get the bottle of Fountain of Youth water before sweet Bella and the youthful pickpocket. So why are time travelers Marty Melbourne and Master Simon interested?

Kidnapped! (Book Eleven) The Scottish police officer would do anything to get his wife back...even trust the mysterious letter sent to him from his ancestor, a convict on The First Fleet into Australia!

Big Mac: (Book Twelve) Fate and science said they should never have met but after that first touch, he knew he'd stay with her forever. Would the sudden appearance of the father he never knew be their doom – and the start of a pandemic?

CONTEMPORARY NOVELLAS – BENJI, THE LOST YEARS
Pool Boy Wanted: No Experience Preferred: (rather racy) Young Benji has been a hostage and slave, but life gets worse when an older woman decides she wants him as her own.

Luke the Unexpected: Love of classic motorcycles brought them together, but Luke and Holly have other challenges to face. Find out how their friend Benji got his stripes here.

STAND ALONE NOVELLAS (contemporary romances)

Kit Kringle: An Alaskan Tale: Kay moved to Alaska for the wrong reasons, then decided to stay and start her own business. What she hadn't planned on were prejudices and falling in love.

Be My Angel: Wyatt's dream to help save the wild mustangs began with the purchase of a rundown ranch in western Oregon. What he hadn't anticipated was being mesmerized by a sassy woman in a wheelchair.

Three Are One: The post chaplain tried to help the young widow adjust, but would his feelings for her and the search for his lost sister cause problems?

One Arctic Summer: That unforgettable summer of 1994 in Barrow, Alaska, and the touch she never forgot…If she goes back, will he remember her?

The Polar Xpress: Will the California chiropractor get a first chance at romance with the owner of Second Chance Kennels when he is stranded in Alaska?

Too Fast For You: Ten years after Little League, two talented professional baseball players wind up on the same minor league team. Will she remember him? And will their friendship be ruined if she does?

A Plate of Christmas Cookies: World War Two got between them the first time around. Would his children prevent him from having a second chance at happiness?

The Wizard of Odds: Four unlikely friends are challenged with making a profit out of an odd lot of unique animals. Can they do it without clobbering each other first? A Romantic Comedy

TRIPLETS: THREE AREN'T ONE (A potpourri of literary styles, all with strong characters)

The Set Up: Grace's story. A gritty women's fiction of how it all began.

<u>Diamonds Aren't for Everyone</u>: Vickie's story. A Billionaire Romance with mysteries and surprises.

<u>That Magic Touch</u>: Ria's story. A tender, heartwarming Medical Romance.

<u>How Love Grows</u>: Tori's story. A spunky young woman insists on doing everything her way. Romantic Comedy.

<u>They Call Me Sherlock</u>: Silas's story. A Romantic Comedy with a touch of time travel.